Mountain Shadow

Memories

JOE COBB CRAWFORD

Mountain Shadow Memories
Copyright @ 2013 Joe Cobb Crawford. All rights reserved.
Cover Photographs by David Greear.
Painting copies by Ken Woodall.
Manuscript edited by John A. Shivers.
Cover design by David Greear.
Type and layout by Dianne VanderHorst.
Published by Laurel Mountain Press
P.O. Box 1973 Clayton, Georgia 30525
laurelmountainpress@windstream.net.

Printed in the United States of America
ISBN: 978-0-9888374-1-6

*Oh Lord, I'm strivin',
tryin' to make it through this barren land,
but as I go from day to day,
I can hear my Savior say,
"trust me child, come on and hold my hand."*

- Lyrics from the song "Rough Side Of The Mountain"

TO
THOSE WHO PRESERVE
AND SHARE THE
HISTORY OF NORTHEAST GEORGIA:

THE NORTHEAST GEORGIA
HISTORY CENTER
GAINESVILLE, GEORGIA

Author's Note

Mountain Shadow Memories is a collection of short stories and tall tales. Some have been told at family gatherings for decades. Friends from the Tri-state area of Georgia, Tennessee, and North Carolina are my source for these stories.

The people of this area are predominantly of Scots-Irish descent. They are people of faith and often hold conservative views on society. They have a history of loving art, music, poetry, and yes, making, selling, and drinking liquor.

The characters portrayed in these stories were often their own worst enemies. They were slaves of their passions, and they lived life to its fullest; they bloomed where they'd been planted, and were never boring.

Those who write on history or anthropology are often asked, "Is the presented information 'true?'" My short answer is: "Absolutely NOT." No person can know past people's truths. We can only try to understand that truth, given their circumstances. As a poet friend once told me, "people are so different and each reads and interprets truth based on where they've come from."

I'm not cynical of History, only Historicists. History is the land of shadows and Historicists create clouds. Historical accounts are, at best, futile attempts to explain man's foibles. History's theme is: humans make mistakes - authors included. As author Robert Byrne put it, "Until you walk a mile in another man's moccasins, you can't imagine the smell."

I come from Southern Appalachia. I hope you enjoy reading our brand of "almost true" stories about the lost past.

Table of Contents

Art List	iii
Prologue	v
Acknowledgments	viii
DRESS	3
COWBOY	21
DINNER	31
BURIED	47
RELATIVES	57
LIGHTNING	67
MILKLESS	75
POKER	89
DISPLACED	109
SNOWBIRDS	129
GONE	141
BOUNDEN	151
About The Author	164
About The Artist	166
Other books by Author	169

Art List

Painting	Story Title	Page
Pa Wright, Old Blue And Red	DRESS	1
Hoppy Comes To Town	COWBOY	19
Dinner Memories	DINNER	29
Sign Man	BURIED	45
Tipton	RELATIVES	55
That Mule, Old Pa Wright And Me	LIGHTNING	65
The Vet	MILKLESS	73
Fields Of The Woods	POKER	87
Midget Wrestlers	DISPLACED	107
Christmas	SNOWBIRDS	127
First TV	GONE	139
Pious Pup	BOUNDEN	149

Picture	Story Title	Page
Joe Tipton	RELATIVES	63
Dot And Al	BOUNDEN	163

Prologue

I am a product of the mountains. Those hills and hollows were a crucible for my coming of age. My values, beliefs, and faith were first known there. Southern Appalachia is in my bones, and droplets from her cool trout streams are in my blood. Like the Psalmist, I often lift my eyes to the mountains and know where my help comes from - from God of course, but from God through the influence of mountain people. Often I pilgrimage there to ensure that I don't lose my bearings, or "get above my raisen."

Strangers visiting the mountains today find their stay pleasant. Contemporary amenities and accommodations abound. For myself, visits are painful and sad, but always cathartic. Like other visitors, when I breathe in the familiar mountain air, I always feel restored physically, spiritually, and emotionally.

The pain alluded to stems from seeing the erosion of mountain culture. The confluence of convenient access and progress are steadily supplanting a past way of life. Sadness, also, because I strongly feel that visitors to the mountains discount or have a jaded perspective of past mountain ways. To some, experiencing mountain culture is little more than a theme park adventure.

By mountain ways I do not reference the "Foxfire" ways so thoroughly documented, but the ways of the second half of the last century. Visitors and recent mountain transplants lack knowledge of the poverty and the harshness of life that accompanied it during this era. Hopefully, the stories in this book will provide insight into the lives of everyday human beings; those non-epic characters who eked out a meager living in the mountains in the second half of the twentieth century.

Mountain poverty was as ugly as a fat tick on a skinny dog, and few will talk about it. Both those seeking to be informed, and the actual trench dwellers from past wars on poverty, cringe, when the subject is mentioned. True mountain people would never tell you they were ever deprived of anything. Mountain folks are a poor, but proud people, and are linguistically reserved. But to discount and not consider poverty's prevalence in the mountains of the last half century is to not know the origin or evolution that continues to transform the mountain culture. The trail leading from poverty is dotted with artifacts suggesting a unique human struggle occurred. Tall tales of tragedy and triumph, sorrow and joy, have marked this trail fomented by poverty. These artifacts are the framework of my stories.

The folk stories found within are about real people, warts and all. Time has changed culture in the mountains, but the characters remain in the minds of Southern Appalachian people. My wish is that they will remain in your mind as well... the characters of my Mountain Shadow Memories.

Acknowledgments

One of the blessings granted a book author is the opportunity to remember and to formally acknowledge people who have helped them along the way. Like most people of Southern Appalachia, those people for me were my family, classmates, and friends. They were in fact, the material source for most of my stories. Others were recalled while writing this book. To these I owe my heart-felt appreciation:

To members of The Toccoa Literary and Chicken Pot Pie Society for their patience in weekly critiquing my writing craft and art. To Society leader and author Lawrence Wertan, for his guidance and irreverent sense of humor. Although he's a 'lowlife flatlander' from Charleston and, like Conroy, he "wears the ring," his leadership kept me on track, sane, and laughing.

I'm also indebted to the group on Facebook called "The Poetry Company Readers." Members of this group encouraged me and kept me going when I'd convinced myself I was no longer a writer. Their continued words of support and feedback on my posted snippets proved critical to this book going to print.

Many others have helped me on my journey along the rough side of the mountain. Some are deceased. Some are characters found in the stories of this book. To all of them, I owe my gratitude and remembrance.

Well, things that happen in the mountains are never what they seem, especially those things that happen in a mountain church.

 # DRESS

The day Uncle Arthur shot and killed Dolphus at Sugar Creek Church is the same day he started wearing that dress. His mama's dress fit him fine, as did the corset, sun bonnet, and lace-up, high-heeled boots. Arthur was in no way effeminate, but was small in frame and stature, like his maternal Ralston side of the family. Endowed with kind blue eyes, lively dark hair, and symmetrical facial features, Arthur's disguise was perfect. But why, of all days and of all places, had he chosen a church on this summer Sunday to come out and tread the boards of Boardtown, Georgia?

Well, things that happen in the mountains are never what they seem, especially those things that happen in a mountain church. Let me explain.

Sugar Creek Church was where Arthur had married his wife, Laura Ward. They regularly attended Sunday services there following their marriage. Laura was an attractive lady and had "sparked" many young gentlemen before marrying Arthur. One such "sparker" was Dolphus Sisson, a man who was the antithesis of Arthur Thomas. Dolphus was rude, crude, and as big as a barn in all directions - personal qualities sometimes needed for survival in the rural north Georgia mountains of 1904.

Dolphus and his brother sat directly behind Arthur and Laura in church that morning. During the services, Dolphus stuck Laura with a large pin thrust through the cracks in the pew slats. Aware of the wrongful act, Arthur turned in the pew, cut his eyes at Dolphus, and short-shook his head. Arthur couldn't speak clearly because of a speech impediment that made him self-conscious. He avoided speaking whenever possible, and often gestured instead. Dolphus relented, until just minutes before the benediction, when he again pierced Laura with the pin.

Laura muffled her scream, causing fellow worshippers to misread her squelched reaction. "A worshipper has just got religion and is filled with the Holy Spirit," they collectively reasoned. One caught up worshipper shouted, "Amen! Bless her Lord." The preacher at the pulpit saw all and sensed such was not exactly the case. Liturgy ceased and he called the benediction. Church was quickly dismissed and all worshippers, except for the feuding four, went home.

If the good reverend thought benediction would make everything right, he was wrong. First, Dolphus made fun of Arthur's troubled talk. Redressing and avenging the wrongs began; fists flew fast and furiously. Arthur was no match for the larger man. After being knocked down, Arthur was lifted and held aloft by Dolphus's brother, while Dolphus continued to work over the seemingly defeated, smaller man. Arthur's battered body finally fell to the ground after a crashing blow smashed and dislodged his nose. Crying loudly, Laura ran to her battered husband, who would accept no comfort.

Blotting blood onto the sleeve of his white shirt, Arthur pushed Laura away, while a weary but confident Dolphus swaggered off, presuming himself the victor. Arthur struggled to lift himself. He staggered, stumbling toward their buggy, where he stealthily removed a loaded shotgun. Through blurred eyes, Arthur took aim, cocked the hammer, and pulled the trigger. Dolphus had turned his head when he heard the gun cock, but his bolt for church refuge wasn't successful. Dolphus lay dead in the vestibule. His brother had been wiser, and fled for his life, seeking cover in the leafy mountain surroundings.

Threshing underbrush was peppered by Arthur, but the assistant assailant escaped. Arthur returned to the buggy, where Laura tried to help him onto the seat, but the proud little man still refused her efforts. As Arthur slouched into the buggy seat, their gray mare flinched and her ears flexed and pointed skyward. The clarion call of a distant train whistle resonated through the hills and hollers surrounding Sugar Creek Church.

Laura grabbed the reins that rippled and snapped along the horse's back, as she screeched a frightful, "HE AH! GET UP, NELL!"

"Oh my Lord, son, what's happened to you?" Arthur's mama, Lealer, cried out in horror, when she saw Arthur hobble toward the front porch of his boyhood homeplace.

Fearing the revenge that might be waiting at their home, Laura had driven Arthur to his parents instead. An armed and angry Sisson clan could be waiting for them at their place, or of equal peril, the Fannin County High Sheriff. Either way, she wasn't taking any chances.

A battered and bloody Arthur, holding his lifeless arm close to his ribcage, struggled up the steps. He eased onto a porch bench.

"John! John, come here quick!" Lealer screamed to her husband through the screen door. "Arthur's been hurt. Hurry, John! Come here!"

John flung open the door and hurried to his son. "Who did this to you, boy?" he demanded.

Arthur didn't respond, as was his nature because

of his speech impediment. Laura spoke instead. She explained the whole story of what had taken place at Sugar Creek Church. Horrified though she was, Lealer was a mama first. She ran to the back porch, poured well water in the wash pan and returned to clean Arthur's wounds. When she was finished, she poured turpentine on the cuts.

Meanwhile John was quickly assessing Arthur's situation. Immediately he saw the few possibilities available for his son's survival, and didn't mince words. "Son, you're going to have to leave this country and soon. There's no other way. If you stay here, you'll be killed by those Sisson folks. They'll hunt you down like a dog and kill you. The crooked law here in Fannin County may even help them. Neither one will be satisfied until you're dead. We've got to figure a way to hide you, then get you to the folks over in Rome, Georgia. You can stay there for a spell, 'til this thing blows over."

A plan was devised for Arthur's seclusion and deliverance. Few from the large Thomas family were privy to the execution of the escape plan, except for Laura, Lealer, John, and Arthur's older and much larger half-brother, Julius. The fewer who knew, the better.

"Mama, I'm a man. I ain't gonna wear that dress," Arthur groaned and moaned, trying to articulate a protest through his cleft palate.

"Son, it's the only way you'll live to see another day," Lealer pleaded, the tears welling up in her eyes. "Now, I know you don't like it none, but you've got to commence wearing this dress." Arthur finally relented, acquiescing in his mom's words. In her heart, although she kept the truth to herself, she knew Arthur would be gone for more than just a few days.

Laura was more concerned with Arthur's immediate danger. She, too, had considered the possibilities for Arthur and their marriage. This could be the last time she would see her husband. Plans they had made to farm and raise a family together were clouded now. Arthur's act of violence had changed everything for them.

The getaway plan was quite simple. Arthur would dress as a woman. Julius would pose as Arthur's husband. Together, they would board a train in Ellijay, Georgia and travel as man and wife to Rome, Georgia. The dress was black and included an optional black veil. They were ostensibly traveling to a funeral. But first, they had to get to the train station for their Monday morning departure. Being recognized was their greatest threat. If discovered, both might be reported, arrested or possibly killed. "A search party or a lynch mob may already be lookin' for you," John admonished.

Fully dressed, with exception of the high heels and veil, Arthur and Julius hid in the hayloft. Neither the law nor the Sisson folks would find them, they reasoned. His mama's corset, though painful at first, actually helped support Arthur's cracked ribs. After midnight, Arthur and Julius would begin their walk. This "funeral march" included a ten mile stretch of railroad tracks through the deepest and darkest hollers in the Southern Blue Ridge Mountains. The trek ran from near Boardtown, Georgia to the train station in Ellijay. Later, as they neared civilization again, Arthur would change into the high heels and add the veil. Fine feminine foot-wear and veiled vision were worthless on the treacherous trails and railroad cross ties the wounded Arthur Thomas would negotiate this late summer night of 1904.

The night Arthur put asunder his bride, his family, and all familiar friends and places in Fannin County was a night of horror. Finding a more solitary and frightful scene than the shadowed mountain rails of steel would be hard to find. Julius and his "leading lady" trod south on those tracks and into a dark wilderness. They knew not, exactly, from whom they were escaping, but knew only that if caught, they would probably be hanged, shot or maybe both. Georgia mountain justice was never deliberated, delayed nor denied, when "reckoned right."

The rail tracks were walled off between a blue chain-link fence of mountains. On the left and on the right, each pierced the sky, blocking light from both moon and stars, and hedging all peripheral vision. This slim trench of a gutter closed in on them, drawing itself about Arthur and Julius like a hangman's noose. The rigid rails at foot converged and pointed in only one direction: toward Arthur's survival. They were the footprint of Arthur's destiny. Few bends in those footprints obscured the fate that awaited them, but an odd mix of plant life impaired their horizon and kept their destiny a mystery. Creek crossings and scattered small vistas of farm meadows and eye-high corn fields yielded no reprieve; only more dreaded death traps to worry about. Pine-thickets, glades of mountain laurel, and tangled alder bushes, all suitable to support a hideout and ambush, further thwarted the brothers' perspective, all that they couldn't see prompted wary peeks, followed by a growing weariness. Strong hilltop oaks and beech trees capable of supporting 'strange fruit' upstaged their escape. Arthur and Julius hoped to not become the strange fruit hanging from those giant trees. Like Lady Justice, these giants would be blind to the meaning of the moment, or to any bravery played out before them, until the cast had completed its walk down.

Nearby, shaded stumps and bark strips soaked, fermenting and souring the musty midnight air. Also garnishing the runway was an occasional cow or hog carcass. These free-range, free-thinking animals had failed to yield to a higher power, namely a locomotive. The train's cowcatcher had carried them before plowing them aside like the garbage they were. Tonight, the swine and bovine's only legacy was a rancid stench that assaulted the brothers' olfactory senses. The deceased, baked by the summer sun, simmered and stewed there on a platter of rusty tracks, rotting crossties, on a rough and rocky road bed. Wind currents were void, stifled by the cooked collage of clutter. Holding heat, they displaced any cool, fresh air that may have stole-away between the folds of the sheltering mountains. Putrid nauseating air hung low to the tracks, giving no comfort to the "lady" who trod the boards in a full-length dress.

On this dark retreat even familiar sounds of the mountains were hushed, haunting, and forlorn. Critters could be heard, but only faintly and were never seen. It was as though all, including the panther whose cry could un-nerve any man, had been told to keep quiet and stay out of sight. Only the call from a whippoorwill could be heard with clarity, but he, too, was never near. The eeriness set the senses of both Arthur and Julius on edge, even without the angst of knowing possible pursuers might attack and kill them at any moment. Like two dogs on the hunt, their primeval instincts prevailed against the horror of this night. God's providence, and not the intellect of a female impersonator, delivered the two hapless young men. Brothers Arthur and Julius Thomas marched from the shadow of death on that sultry summer night in 1904.

Breakfast eggs had not yet cracked back at the Thomas house before Julius stood on the platform of the train station waiting to buy tickets. He'd left Arthur behind, secluded at the woods' edge of Ellijay. Two one-way tickets to Rome Georgia would be purchased, but only if Julius didn't recognize anyone at the station. Only then would he return for their luggage, and escort his incognito lady in mourning to the station, while goods were off-loaded from the train and new supplies, water, mail and baggage were muscled onto the train.

While in wait, Arthur would change into his full travel attire. His brogans would be replaced with the laced up high heels and the sunbonnet would be replaced with a black Edwardian hat and veil. A matching parasol had been available, but her ladyship had strongly demurred, feeling it made him look like a strumpet. The accepted veil proved vital to the disguise. No one had thought to consider the dark black stubble that now shadowed the face of the bereaved "lady."

Fate was friendly on this muggy Monday morning. Julius had seen only strangers at the train station. He bought the tickets and then proceeded to "cherchez la femme." He found Arthur exactly where he'd left him, sprawled out, back against an oak tree, resting. They stayed at the woods' edge until the train's whistle announced its approach to the station. Then, arm in arm, Julius escorted "her" at first on tippy-toes and then with normal steps, down the tracks to a road crossing. From there, they promenaded a red dirt road to the station and boarded the train to Rome and the Davis relatives.

Their Davis relatives sheltered both young men for a week. Convinced that the Sissons or the Fannin County law would soon hunt Arthur down and avenge

Dolphus' death, Julius and Arthur devised a plan to get farther away from Fannin County. They would go west, but where in the west?

Rome, Georgia was a booming crossroads in the fourth year of the century. Travelers and railway workers frequently passed through the town. Talk was that a little town north of Dallas, Texas, a place called 'Sunset' was hiring railway workers. Coincidentally, Arthur's deceased uncle, Joseph, had children living in Sunset, Texas. The destination was set. Using the same disguise and personas, the young men would travel to Sunset, Texas.

Boarding the train in Rome, for Sunset, were a couple by name of Mr. and Mrs. Julius Thomas. Arriving in Sunset, were two young men named Julius Thomas and William Fain. Julius returned immediately to Fannin County Georgia, but Arthur, aka, William Fain, remained to begin a new life under a new name. The name was a combination of his grandfather William Thomas and Fain, the maiden name of his grandmother. William Fain would be his name for the remainder of his tormented life.

William Fain worked for the railroad company only a short time. He quickly became part of his new world. He had been known in Fannin County as skilled with horses. He brought these skills from the Georgia mountains with him to Texas.

Texans valued horses only slightly less than family. William understood horses and could break and train them better than a seasoned Texas cowhand. Unlike his human counterparts, horses clearly heard and understood his flawed mutterings. Trading, breeding, and training horses would become William Fain's life's work in his new land.

Laura never joined Arthur in Texas and everyone wondered why. Many concluded Arthur had died or had been killed. The true reason was never known. What was known with certainty, however, was that neither Laura nor any family member ever revealed Arthur's whereabouts. For years, the few informed family members lived in fear. Rumors and unrequited mountain justice lingered in Fannin County, and the law repeatedly sought leads regarding Arthur's escape.

On the other hand, the locals of the bustling town of Sunset, Texas were never curious about the young, cautious man. His partially paranoid behavior fit into the wild-west culture of Texas like a new boot fit in an old stirrup. His ever-present, strapped-on Colt Peace Maker also caused no alarm. Even his "Wild Bill Hickok" seating preference in public places, with his back to a wall, iron un-tethered and windows and doors scanned, was apropos in early twentieth century Texas.

William Fain's first few years in Texas were hard, lonely and frightful times. Returning home to his bride, family and friends was never to be. Young William accepted this cold fact. He knew the day he set foot in Fannin County would be the same day he sucked in his last breath of mountain air. In time, William Fain moved on with his second life.

His cousins in Texas introduced him to a Mary Anne "Mollie" Niece. They soon married and started a family. Unknown to William Fain was that Mollie was not a native Texan. She had only lived there thirteen years. Like William, she too, had roots in Georgia. At age nine her family had moved from Ivy Log, Georgia, a small community bordering William's home county of Fannin. Neither of their families had known each other back in North Georgia.

Together, William and Mollie raised six children. Twelve were born to the couple, but only six had lived. Infant mortality was common in the early twentieth century. The ever-cautious William supported his family with money he earned in the horse and mule trading business.

Many years following their marriage, William happened to visit the Sunset, Texas train station where he had first arrived so many years before. He'd gone there on business regarding horses he'd soon ship down to San Antonio. It was there, standing on the station platform, that William Fain saw what he thought must be a ghost from the past. A large, young man, appearing something less than twenty years of age, stood there, looking down the tracks. He held a strange object in his hand. Images of Dolphus and that horrible day at Sugar Creek Church raced through William's mind. This hulk of a youngster spotted William and slowly made his way toward him. Holding out an outdated and faded black parasol, the young man simply said, "Here, Daddy. You left this back at home."

Daddy or no one else ever believed me, but it's the gospel truth. I saw a cowboy wearing a black hat get killed that day.

# COWBOY

"He wore a black hat, Tommy."

It was late afternoon and the man and boy were the only two humans in sight, among a sea of granite and marble. Tommy's grand-paw winced as he uttered the words in a loud whisper, and a shadowy silence hovered over them. Together, they stared at a faded red rock nearby. A hesitant sun started its descent behind the Blue Ridge Mountain range, and grand-paw touched Tommy's shoulder, then twirled his white mustache with the fingers of his other hand. As though he'd seen a ghost, he mumbled, "I remember the last time I saw that black hat. It's as clear in my mind today as it was sixty years ago."

"But Paw, if he was a cowboy, what was he doing here? I thought cowboys and Indians all lived out west. Was he a bad guy?"

"Well, Tommy, ordinarily cowboys do live out west, but this unlucky cowboy hankered to roam. He was from Oklahoma and, as far as I know, he wasn't an outlaw. He was just trying to find his roots."

"His roots? What's you talking about, Paw?" Don't they have roots out west?"

The sun retreated behind Big Frog Mountain. Twilight crept in, but the birds didn't stop chirping. Tommy's grand-paw studied their noise. Then, as though he'd awakened from a dream, he spoke, quietly, hesitantly at first, before warming to his subject. The story he told had taken place in the Tennessee border town known as McCaysville, Georgia.

"It was 19 ought 2. I was about your age, Tommy. We lived on the Georgia side of the river. Back then, a lot of people worked for the Tennessee Copper Company. You know, where those mining rigs are, across the Ocoee River in Tennessee? They mined lots of copper way back then. Lots of men worked underground in the mines. My daddy wasn't a miner, but a miner told him about the cowboy. Daddy, he never put much stock in the story, 'cause miners was bad to drank liquor and sometimes they'd tell stuff that weren't true."

"And he wore a black hat?" Tommy confirmed.

"Yep. A big-brimmed black hat, and he just wandered in late one afternoon, into a bar over near Ducktown, Tennessee. Wanted a cold beer and some directions. Passing through on his way to North Carolina, he said. He was trying to find a little community across the state line near Murphy called Bloody Bucket, where he was supposed to have family. The bartender asked him if he was an Indian, because a few Indians had settled in Bloody Bucket, and still lived there. It was an obvious question, given this man's dark skin. But there was no answer from the black-hatted stranger. Instead, he told the bartender he had ridden his horse, called her Soquili, for forty straight miles without stopping to sleep. He explained he'd followed the river upstream through the mountains on the Old Copper Road.

"Many miners back then, Tommy, were hard working people, but when they weren't working, they liked to drank, and carouse and get in trouble. Some of the miners at the bar saw the black hat, the stranger's rattlesnake boots and spurs, and decided to have some fun. After all, he weren't nothing more than a half-breed Indian and a stranger to boot.

"One miner slipped outside to check out the horse story. 'Soquili', it turned out, was a magnificent animal; a red roan, eighteen hands high and built for running. She was tied to the hitching post out front of the Three Bears Trading Post. A noosed lariat and a leatherbag hung from the saddle, and the miner made it his business to snoop. His reward, in a pouch inside the saddlebag, was a piece of paper with an Oklahoma City, Oklahoma address. With it also was a picture of an old Indian woman.

"We got us a genuine Indian cowboy here fellers," shouted the snooping miner as he re-entered the bar. Laughing as he waved the picture of the old Indian woman, he demanded, "Tell me mister, are you an Indian or are you a cowboy?"

The stranger didn't respond, but turned quietly and left the bar. "Tommy, those drunk miners shouted bad things at him and called him names. In a flash the stranger swung into his saddle and he and Soquili galloped off.

"One drunk miner belted out a challenge: 'Five dollars to the man who catches that Indian and brings me that black hat he's wearing.' Three sober miners took the dare, mounted their mules, and the chase was on.

"The stranger was smart. He tried to throw his pursuers off track by taking another route. He turned south at 'Five Points' and took the road to Copperhill, Tennessee and McCaysville, Georgia. Soquili ran like the wind. The mule-riding miners were left behind. The cowboy was relieved to leave his pursuers. He continued to look over his shoulder because he had entered a strange land. Though dusky dark, he saw a sight most bizarre to his thinking. Spread out before his eyes was a land with no green plants. Only bare, red-gutted hills greeted him. And the air smelled terrible, much like rotting eggs or rancid hay. Soquili abandoned her run with the wind and began gasping instead for air. The cowboy slowed her to a walk, enabling her to catch her breath, since his pursuers were nowhere in sight. Approaching the town of Copperhill, the cowboy discovered the source of the stink - a hulking, rusty structure that belched orange colored gases.

"Then, out of nowhere, his pursuers appeared again, Tommy. 'Stop that Injun cowboy,' they yelled for anyone who would listen. He robbed the Three Bears Trading Post.' An old apron-draped merchant looked up, but made no move to stop the cowboy. The Edward's Ferry attendant heard the cries, too, but he ignored the commotion.

"Sensing his pursuers had him cornered at the ferry crossing, the cowboy goosed Soquili, who galloped down the riverbank and into the chilly waters of the Ocoee River. Together they swam toward Georgia. One of the miners realized that the cowboy was getting away, and fired a lethal shot that found itself at home in the majestic steed. Soquili squealed once, flopped, then floated lifelessly down stream. Holding the black hat in one hand, the cowboy dove deep, and let the swift current carry him downstream. He emerged, placed the black hat on his head, and raced into McCaysville.

"But the miners didn't give up. By now it was a matter of pride and they didn't intend to lose. The ferry attendant had transported them to the Georgia side of the river and, once again, the rabbit was in their sight and the chase was on. The stranger ran for his life up Tater Hill. In Kingtown, where my family lived when I was your age, Tommy, they caught up with him. My parents were gone, and I was in the barn milking Bessie, when the cowboy appeared. He stood at the entrance to our barn, dripping wet, wearing that big, wilted black hat. Scared the devil out of me, he did. Bessie was scared too and danced sideways, kicking over a bucket full of milk.

"He was a stark figure in the black hat and he stood stock still, pleading 'Where can I hide! They're trying to kill me!" Before I could tell him to climb to the hayloft, I heard a shot. The cowboy fell face down in the barnyard. Shot in the back, there he lay, dead. I scampered up the ladder to the loft. Within seconds, one miner rode up on a lathered-up bay mule. Peeping down from overhead, I saw him dismount and pick up the black hat. Scared stiff, I lay forever under the hay, waiting...

"What happened to the evening milk?" It was mama's voice I finally heard, as I lay trembling under the hay and I knew she was angry. Even in my half-awake stupor, I knew she was angry. With light from her lantern, I climbed down from the loft.

"He's dead, Mama! They shot him and took his black hat."

"Shot who?" Mama demanded. "Who are you talking about and why is there milk everywhere? Did you spill the milk again?"

"No, Ma'am! Bessie did it. The cowboy scared her."

"Cowboy my hind foot!" she scolded. "Do you see a cowboy here anywhere?"

"I had to admit I didn't."

She grabbed me by my shoulder. "Come on. It's late. Let's get to the house. You can tell your daddy about this in the morning."

"I slept none that night because that dead cowboy's image lingered in my mind, even with my eyes screwed tight shut." He stopped talking, and Tommy saw his grand-paw going to a place he couldn't see. Then, as suddenly as he stopped, grand-paw began speaking again. "Some nights still, when I can't sleep, I see him. When morning came, I told daddy about it, but he didn't believe me. Laughed at me, he did.

"Tell ya what, son," he said, 'I'll check on that dead cowboy on my way to the outhouse. Wait here 'til I get back.' When he returned, he was still laughing. 'No dead cowboy in the barn,' he announced.

"A few days later daddy heard about an out-of-state Indian stopping in at the Three Bears Trading Post, but he still didn't believe me.

"Weeks passed. Then, an unmarked grave was discovered here in Kingtown Church's cemetery. 'That's it right there, Tommy.' Grand-paw pointed toward the faded red rock.

"That's the headstone, Tommy. That's his headstone, the cowboy who wore that black hat. I put that stone there myself, about sixty year ago, it was. Daddy or no one else ever believed me, but it's the gospel truth. I saw a cowboy wearing a black hat get killed that day."

"I believe you, Paw. I believe you."

*Regardless of what
was required,
they had sworn
to never go hungry
on Sundays.*

 # DINNER

The Great Depression years were hard and hungry times. Life languished like a bad case of the itch, testing body, spirit, and soul. Nowhere was this more prevalent than in the Great Copper Basin straddling the Georgia-Tennessee line. Young people there were confronted daily with harsh realities of economic hardship. While some youth pretended immunity to their poverty, others chose fancy over fact, in order to cope with these wanting times. Innocent charades and capers were common. A fraction of the youth were even militant, and they defied their wretched state by engaging in Robin Hood-inspired escapades.

Four such youths were the "Sunday Dinner Bunch" or the "S. Debees" as they fancied themselves. Regardless of what was required, they had sworn to never go hungry on Sundays. A blood drop on a shag smoke paper had documented each member's pledge. The oaths were kept in a bright red Prince Albert Tobacco can. Only Fred Hamby, the S. Debees' self-appointed commander of their ad hoc band, knew the whereabouts of said documents.

Sunday dinner on this particular Sabbath would be hosted at the home of one Rupert Pembroke, a pillar of the community and head of an ostensibly affluent family from the Great Basin. The Pembrokes were said to be well off, and their brick home attested to that fact. Like a castle, their host's home overlooked the Ocoee River, and was ever-visible from Hendrixtown, a poor community of rental row houses. Unlike Mr. Pembroke, most people living in Hendrixtown were day-pay employees for The Company, a copper processing plant.

Workers had long earned a living wage for their families from The Company. Now, however, times were tough. The fat of the land had turned skinny and ugly. Most workers were limited to earning only one or two days a week in wages. Wages that barely bought food for a small family. Larger families fared worse. Children in those homes often went to bed hungry.

The Pembroke family was not adversely affected by the Great Depression. Mr. Pembroke, unlike most, had a good, steady salary. They were religious people and regularly attended Sunday services. After the morning service, they always returned home to a sumptuous dinner, which Mrs. Pembroke cooked before leaving for church. Today, however, their Sunday ritual would be derailed.

"Company halt!" Fred commanded, as he peered about the bare red hills of the Great Copper Basin. A screen door slammed nearby, causing a dog in the distance to bark. "At ease men. Take one knee. Roll your smokes if you got 'em," Fred ordered. Then he sucked in a deep breath of morning's misty air.

"Hey, Ab, you got any more of that rabbit 'backer left?" The gruff question came from Harry Hamby, Fred's older brother. "I got a piece of the Sunday funny papers from th' outhouse. We can roll us a smoke with it if you got 'backer."

"Naw, I ain't got none. Smoked it all yesterday," Ab Winslow answered. He was a shy but determined boy from Hendrixtown.

"How bout you, Eddie? You got any 'backer?" This time it was Eddie Swartz, a pensive teen from across the river in Copperhill, that Harry hit on.

Eddie ignored him, almost as if the question had never been broached.

Suddenly, the sound of church bells stung their ears, and their need to smoke was forgotten. Ten peals resonated up the river and echoed throughout the Basin. They echoed through the rusty steel canyons of the copper plant, and floated in the fog above the red gullies. Absent today, however, was the rumble and roar of clattering machinery. Also missing was the sulfur-soaked air. The Company was a sleeping mechanical giant, shut down and lifeless. On Tuesday the giant would reawaken, and normal life would return. The plant would then run two days to process their meager copper orders, before going into hibernation once again.

"Okay, guys," Fred announced. "You hear

them church bells? We got just a little over an hour to complete our mission. When that bell rings again, we've got to be finished and gone. Is everyone clear on that? Like I told you before, take nothing, leave nothing. Now, let's move. Company forward!"

They skulked into the yard of the immaculately landscaped home and quickly followed a gravel path to the rear of the house, out of sight of the road. A tiny square door at the base of the house was their destination. Fred had identified it during earlier reconnaissance. The door covered a chute used to deliver coal into the basement. Unlike most houses in the GCB, the Pembroke home had ultra-modern central heating.

"Like I told you, guys, slide head first down this coal chute," Fred advised. "I'll help each of you. At the bottom there's a coal bin. Light a match soon as you land, so we can see our way to the upstairs."

Fred held each man's feet as the member lay head down in the chute and, at just the right moment, released him to slide down into the bowels of the house. The S. Debees rumbled down the chute and crashed hard into the pile of coal at the bottom. Evidently a new shipment had recently been received. Then Fred entered the chute himself and slid quickly into the basement.

He meticulously picked at a splinter he had picked up from his trip down the wooden passageway.

The other S. Debee members stood stock still, holding high their lit matches, and surveyed their dungeon-like surroundings. Each tried not to look scared. With the splinter removed, Fred lit his own match, assumed a more casual attitude and, in a voice grand with expression, announced, "Gentlemen, would you please follow me to the top of these stairs. Once there, you will savor a delightful assortment of cuisine the chef has prepared just for members of the S. Debee." In the flickering light, each man cast a questioning eye at the coal smudged faces of the others. Without saying it, each wondered if they'd be caught.

Then Harry growled, "Let's go, fellers. I'm hungry as a bitch wolf."

When they arrived at the top of the steps, Fred quietly cracked open the door, the creak of the hinges shattering an otherwise perfect silence. Spying into the dusky room, he reached around the door jam, found a light switch, and flipped it. Instantly the room was bathed in brightness, thanks to a beautiful chandelier that hung from the center of the tall ceiling. The fixture glistened and glittered, spotlighting a cloth-covered dining table.

"Gentlemen, please wait here while I prepare your places." Fred strutted to the table like a trained maitre d', where he removed the cloth, taking extreme care to fold the piece of damask just so. Each corner was exact. All fold lines were parallel and perpendicular.

Never mind that tell-tale black smudges were evident everywhere he had touched the fabric. He laid the folded cloth across his forearm and tippy-toed toward a large china cabinet. There he carefully placed the folded cloth in a drawer and, with his head held high, he raced to where the others waited.

Approaching Ab, he greeted him. "Mr. Winslow. Please walk this way to the seat we have waiting especially for you."

Ab raised his brow a bit, but toggled his head in agreement. He trotted at Fred's side like a blind pup and took his seat. Sitting quietly wasn't Ab's strong suit, and he took to nervously ringing his filthy little hands, while his hungry belly and overactive imagination anxiously pondered the fine food he was about to devour. He reached a rusty, restless hand toward the relish bowl, only to have Fred instantly slap away the offending member.

"Mr. Winslow! Please! You must wait until all our guests have been seated. I will be serving you three courses for your Sunday dinner, and you will not leave hungry, I promise." Ab's face underwent several odd contortions before, finally, he cocked his head, squinted, and gazed at Fred in half-bewildered agreement.

Next, Fred executed the same procedure for Eddie Swartz, the smallest S. Debee member. Eddie was awestruck by the shiny chandelier. His eyes were fixed on its star-bright sparkle, and he dawdled along behind Fred. His attention upward caused his feet to stumble over the dining room rug. Fred spun around and sneered at Eddie, but said nothing. He shook his head as a condescending expression captured his face. He simply gestured with his hand toward the chair and said, "Puh...leese.....be seated, Mr. Swartz."

Fred returned to the dining room entrance where Harry still waited, impatience clearly written across his face. Harry's eagle-fierce eyes scanned up and down the hallway, his body language screaming his distrust of the whole situation. Then, before Fred could say a word, Harry belted out, "Get out of my way, runt! I'm hungry and I know where I'm going. Sure as heck don't need you to show me how to eat." With that, he shoved Fred aside and made a mad dash toward the dining room, where he dropped into a seat at the end of the long table.

Fred's only response was to flinch and gently roll one shoulder, as he tried to regain command. Struggling with a desire to respond, he trotted instead into the kitchen and returned with a cloth-covered platter of biscuits in one hand, and a dish of butter in the other. He announced, "Would you gentlemen like a dinner roll?" Then he set the butter dish down on the table, and folded back the napkin that covered the perfectly browned biscuits. Harry sprang to his feet and swooped in on the bread. He pounced on two biscuits with one hand, while shoving little Eddie aside with the other hand. Eddie, who had been selectively sorting through the platter in search of the largest biscuits, suddenly found himself coming up short. Fred flashed a fleeting look of displeasure at Harry's crude behavior, but turned on his heel and returned to the kitchen.

In a flash he was back with a rather large bowl and announced, "Gentlemen, the chef has prepared for your dining pleasure his favorite dish. He calls this divine dish 'Candied Yams'".

"I like me some candy," Ab piped up, as the whites of his eyes beamed in contrast to his soot-covered face.

Harry stood up and sternly studied the contents of the bowl. In a surly voice he groused, "Guys, it ain't nothing but danged old sweet taters. That's all it is, sweet taters." Then he wrestled the bowl away from Fred and emptied half the contents onto his plate. "What else they got back there in that kitchen, Fred?" He continued to grumble even as he attacked the potatoes.

Fred took that as his cue and returned to the kitchen where he'd seen other delights. He returned carefully carrying a large platter of fried chicken. Cautiously he sat the platter on the dining table and eased into a chair. All S. Debee members surrounded him like a pack of hungry hyenas. With their forks they stabbed at their prized pieces of chicken. Fred, too, attempted to snare a drumstick, but quickly dropped his fork and pulled back his empty hand, shaking it to be sure it was still intact. Harry had stabbed him.

"I can't take you morons nowhere!" Fred moaned. "You all are so uncouth and ever one of you lacks social graces." Finally he filled his own plate and began to enjoy the Pembroke's delicious Sunday dinner. About half an hour passed and each S. Debee member had stuffed himself. Conversation became confined primarily to grunts, groans, and gestures, interspersed with burps and belches.

"What's for dessert?" The query from little Eddie came in his usual shrill, nasally twang. Eddie had already stashed several biscuits in his pockets, after carefully splitting each one, buttering it, then sprinkling the middles with sugar.

It was with no little effort that Fred lifted his suddenly too-heavy body from the chair, and made his way toward the kitchen. This time, walking with the limp-legged gait of the overfed, he returned with a large bowl of banana pudding. The custard and meringue confection slowly circled the table, as each S. Debee spooned far more than he could ever eat onto his plate. They continued to gorge themselves, as each became even more lethargic, almost to the point of being sick. Clanging utensils ceased and silence reigned. The dining room became library quiet, as each S. Debbee drifted into drowsiness, before finally dozing off.

It was with the ringing of the church bell that roused

them, rudely and without warning, from their slumbers. Twelve bells! They should have already been long gone.

"Hurry, guys!" Fred shouted. "We've gotta skedaddle! They'll be home any time now!"

Each member struggled to stand and leave the table that had served them such a feast. It was with lead-heavy bodies that they lumbered up the hall and descended the steps into the basement. Lighting matches, each helped the other crawl back up the coal chute... back to bitter reality, albeit with full guts.

Harry was the first up and he punched open the coal chute door with the heel of his hand. Then, in alarm, he drew back, after being met with angry amber eyes upstaged by white pointed teeth and pink gums. Goose pimples erupted over his entire body, as a gut-wrenching growl rumbled down the coal chute and landed in the hearts of the guys back in the basement. Sweat beads burst forth on Harry's forehead.

"Get back, guys! Get back! " he screamed. "There's a mean black dog out there and he wants a piece of me for his dinner!"

Like turtles falling off a floating log, the S. Debees plunged back into the coal bin. Fred, wheezing frantically, quickly lit a match. Shadowy, scared faces listened as he demanded, "Okay, guys, listen up. We got to get out of here and quick. One of you will have to face that dog. Who's it going to be?"

"I'm not going out there," was Harry's quick retort. "That dog's after my throat. He'll tear me to bits. You go yourself, Mr. Large-and-In-Charge."

Flailing one arm, Fred insisted, "Forget about what I been doing. We can't stay here, guys. Dog or no dog, we got to get out of here. The Pembrokes will be home any minute. We'll go to jail if they catch us here. So who's it going be?"

Appearing to show almost no concern about the dilemma, little Eddie listened. Silence settled in the dank, dark basement. Breaking the silence, finally, Eddie asked in his grating voice, "Why are we leaving this way? Why don't we go upstairs and walk out the door like normal people would?"

"That's right," Ab seconded. " We could just walk straight out the door. It's locked from the inside and we--."

Fred interrupted. "Shut your yap, Ab. Guys, the plan is to leave the same way we came in. We have no way to lock the door back from the outside. Remember, it's our trademark. We leave the scene clean. It's got to look like a ghost, or even God himself, absconded with the dinner."

Again, Eddie spoke, his voice tinged with obvious reluctance. "Look guys, if we're going to get out of here, we're going to have to change our plan."

"What do you have in mind, Eddie?" Fred's tone was almost pleading.

Eddie laid it out. "Here's what we can do. I'll go to the front door and feed the dog crumbs from one of the biscuits I stashed. I'll keep him distracted, while you all go up the chute and out. When you all are outside, you call the dog to you. I'll stop feeding him and you can start feeding him. Keep him distracted. I'll lock the door, come back here to the basement, and climb out the chute. We'll all meet back at the oak tree. You just be certain that hungry mutt doesn't see me crawl out. Got it?"

"That might just work," Fred agreed, his entire body screaming "relief". "Let's get started."

Eddie pulled a doctored biscuit from his pocket, looked at it longingly, then handed it to Harry, who refused it. "I ain't messing with that dang dog!" he declared. Eddie then offered the dog bait to Fred, who accepted it, but told Eddie in no uncertain terms, "You keep that dog in front of the house, you hear? If you see him turn and go after us, you yell! Do you get me?"

"Got it, Fred," Eddie agreed and then demanded, "You gotta do the same for me. You whistle, or yell, or something, if that mangy mutt b-lines toward the coal chute door."

"You got it, partner," Fred agreed. "Let's move, men!"

Eddie's plan was executed to perfection, almost as though it had been rehearsed a dozen times. After the killer canine had finished eating the sugar biscuit dinner, he licked his lips and lay down for an afternoon nap.

Once all the S. Debees were gathered at the oak tree, they tried to run for safety, but quickly had to coast to a walk. They were nauseated from too much food, followed too quickly by way too much activity. Harry was so sickened, he stepped to the side of the road, placed his hands on his knees and barfed.

Hard hungry times had been defeated--at least for this Sunday. Mission was accomplished. Dog bites were denied thanks to Eddie's daring plan. The S. Debees slouched away single file, and retreated to their pine thicket sanctuary. Once there, Fred passed around a pint of peach brandy he'd pilfered from the Pembroke's pantry. Diligently they deliberated their next.

Oh, who would it be?
The one with the most?
No-R.S.V.P.
Sunday's Dinner Host.

*No one suspects. No one knows
the absolute truths
buried in this graveyard.*

BURIED

It was almost dark when I found the graveyard hidden away on a lonely hill, surrounded by a suffocating forest. The yellow, cold light of the winter sun was fading on the western horizon, as I pushed through the rusted gate. I had walked only a short distance in the rustling leaves, when I heard footsteps behind me. Only when I stopped, the noise stopped.

I looked around. The mournful weeping of the wind was the only sound. I had to hurry, because I didn't want to be in the woods after dark. I moved forward with renewed purpose, looking at the names on the stones and, again, heard steps behind me. I wheeled around, but again, no one was there.

Why had I risked coming to this remote place? "Go home!" I ordered myself. What if my friends see me here? Worse yet, what if someone snaps a picture of me snooping around in a graveyard? Almost at dark no less. "Get a grip on your imagination," I told myself. "You need to confront your fears." I couldn't turn back now. I'd put off dealing with this tormenting albatross for far too long. Maybe I should have at least waited until after sunset, I reasoned. After all, a lady of my social standing does have an image to maintain.

By all outward appearances, I suppose my life has moved on since that tragic day, but appearances are very deceiving. Today, I'm a willing slave on Society Plantation. I have all the perks and status symbols to prove it. My thoughts, not my feelings nor my acts, reveal the true me. Like this graveyard, bounded by a forest, my memories of ten years ago have entrapped me. They haunt me daily. Time hasn't lessened its grip on me, either. Emily Dickinson's poem was spot on: "Time never did assuage." If it did, there was no malady to begin with. Time also, will never assuage my guilt or the malady of his absence from my life. That's why I must do what I fear I cannot.

Turning around I saw an irony to match all ironies: the tombstone of the judge who had sentenced him. To confirm my vision, with my eyes squinted, I stepped closer to his honor's immaculate grave plot. Again, I heard the trailing footstep- a little louder now than before. This time I chose to ignore them. "He's buried here in the same graveyard!" I gasped in disbelief. Palpable feelings of self-righteousness and a warped sense of justice cheered within me. The judge's massive monument was matched only by his well-known intellect and his jumbo ego. He was blissfully ignorant of many things. Now he's buried here along with his ignorance. "Perfect! How fitting! God is a just God," I quipped to myself. The judge was vanity personified, I thought. "Stop smiling!" I ordered myself in the sternest of terms, as a smirk raced across my stinging, wind-chapped lips. "Nice granite epitaph carving too," I groused, while reaching for, then stroking the judge's smooth, icy tombstone.

An aberrant thought flitted through my mind; the sensation of his warm skin once again touching mine. I could smell his cologne. I had buried all those thoughts and feelings after his death, but why had they surfaced again? Here, of all places, in a graveyard? "You are one sick puppy. He's dead!" I chastised myself. Not to worry, I thought. My husband loves me and he suspected nothing ten years ago.

My eyes spied an enormous embossed picture of the robed judge. He looked more arrogant than how I remembered him on that day in court. His pompous, ugly mug was positioned front and center on his glorious tombstone. Consistently pretentious, but a bit much for a tombstone I thought. I also don't think he'll need a robe down there in the place where he (and maybe me, too?) is spending eternity. "Move on!" I demanded of myself.

Chilled by the wind, but now feeling emboldened, I inched and cautiously eased my way down the hill's dark pathway. Judging from the inferior aesthetics of the many shapes ahead, these were the gravestones for people of a lesser God. I was determined to find the place of his interment, the place I had avoided for ten years. "This pilgrimage will finally set me free from my guilt," I told myself. The wind swept through the treetops, howling and whistling, as I crept by the many headstones of the dead. Still, I could hear the sound of footsteps, now even louder and eerily in sync with mine.

Coincidentally, a cold wind had howled also on that last night when we were one. I had felt so warm and loved, wrapped in his arms. It was wrong on so many levels, but then in my life, it had felt so right.

His grave was nothing like that of the man who sentenced him. Existing in a state of abandonment, I finally found it at the graveyard's fringe, out near the tree-line at the base of the hill. Brown leaves covered and accumulated atop his grave plot. With more dark than light now, I saw the nondescript tombstone and made out the faintly legible markings that spelled out his name. So I knelt, touched the tombstone, and traced with my fingers along the weather-worn letters... a name that bore no significance for anyone but me. "I'm so sorry!" I cried out. A gust of wind squelched my anguished words. Soundlessly, my tears crashed and splashed on the musty brown leaves. Those rotting leaves, they hid and harbored the bones of the man I once loved. My husband's best friend.

In our hometown ten years ago, his name was on the mind and lips of everyone. The judge had presided over his trial. Under oath, some had testified about the man they saw run from a murder scene; a man who looked a lot like the person upon whose grave I now spilt tears. To the honorable judge's credit, a fair trial was heard. He had directly asked my lover, "What's your alibi? If you were someplace else, then you won't have to die."

In a crowded courtroom, I sat and watched it all like a deaf mute. He stole a glance at me, but spoke not a word in his own defense. By state law, the judge could, and did, sentence him to death.

No one suspects. No one knows the absolute truths buried in this graveyard. No one knows he was with me that cold, windy night ten years ago; the night someone else ran from the scene of that killing. Things were not clear then. Many things still aren't clear today. I feel like no one knows the real me. Hell-fire, some days I don't know the real me.

Society Plantation, where I've spent my last ten years, buries her truths deep. The deepest buried truth of all is about the cost of honor to a person of valor, and also to a cowardly, willing slave like me. The

Eagles' lyrics are right: Every form of refuge does have its price.

Though I tremble in a cold dark graveyard, I feel better here. I can see some things more clearly from this most unlikely of inspirational surroundings. Three things are perfectly clear to me and I know with certainty these facts are true:

> An innocent man was wrongly sent to his death.
>
> The real killer is still out there somewhere.
>
> Those footsteps I heard- they're gone for now.

*Mountain justice was swift
and lived up to its reputation.*

 # RELATIVES

He was hunting for quail
When the curve ball from hell
Darted and danced his way.

Retribution-
Seemed a just solution
For kindred's loss that day.

"You take one more step and I'll blow your head off!"

The challenge, spoken by the man holding the shotgun, was underscored by the sound of the gun's hammer being cocked.

His target, Joe Tipton, had rounded a rocky bluff high in the Georgia hills, when the gunman and a grassy meadow flashed before him. "Whoa, now! Hold on, mister. Why do you want to shoot me? I've done you no wrong!"

"Reckon we'll see about that," the armed man responded, still holding his bead on Joe's head. "Now you just lay down that gun you're totin', real slow and careful like. As it is, I'm a half-mind to shoot your sorry ass right here and now."

"What've I done, mister?" Joe pleaded, assuming his familiar ball catcher's stance, then softly laying his gun to his side, just as he'd been instructed. You wouldn't kill a man just for trespassing, would you?"

"This ain't 'bout no trespassing, mister. What's your name?"

"Tipton's my name. Joe Tipton."

"Tipton, huh? Are you touched in the head or somethin'? Tipton's MY name." He waggled the barrel of the gun to emphasize that declaration.

"No sir, Mr. Tipton! Honest, my name is Joe Tipton. I got no proof on me, but back at my car I got I.D. I'm a professional baseball player. I'm just out here trying to find a few birds today."

"Hell, you don't look like none of my Tipton kinfolks. You look like a bird yourself. Your eyes is too narry," he bantered, his thumb still nervously fidgeting with the gun's hammer.

"Honest, mister. My name is Joe Tipton. I'm from over at McCaysville. Surely you've heard of me. I play baseball for Cleveland. I was the catcher for the Indians in the World Series this year."

"Cleveland, Georgia or Cleveland, Tennessee?" The man paused as though his mind had wandered to ponder Joe's words. Rage returned from remission, and his eyes glared with hatred. "I 'on't know nothing 'bout no baseball games in Cleveland," he barked.

Joe sensed insanity was on the loose, and feared he'd never be back behind home plate again. Shaking like a leaf in the wind, a spot darkened his crotch. Near tears, he knelt, pleading desperately, "Mr. Tipton, please don't kill me. I've done you no wrong. Please tell me what you think I've done." He struggled for just the right words. "Let me take you to my car. It's...it's back up the trail a ways, but I do have identification there. I can prove I am who I say I am. Please, Mr. Tipton! I've done nothing to you. Please don't shoot me!"

In a split-second, the mountain of a man changed his entire composure. A flicker of compassion glinted in his eyes; a flicker not missed by a player skilled at reading signals and batter apprehension. Tension slacked from the shooter's arm. His shaking support hand dropped from the gun barrel.

"Aw right. Stop your damn whining. Yeah, I seed your car. A black one, weren't it? I guess you think you can drive in these mountains and do anything you want? Well, here's what you gonna do. You empty them shells from that gun of yourn and throw them over here. Then we gonna walk back to that black car."

Joe did exactly as ordered. The man stooped and one-handedly picked up the shells and stuffed them in his coat pocket, all the while still pointing his gun at Joe.

"Now, you walk ahead of me back to that car of yourn. You break and try to run, and I'll blow you clear into kingdom-come. You 'stand what I'm saying, Mr.

Ball Player?

"Yes, sir, Mr. Tipton. I ain't gonna try nothing dumb."

Single file, with the elder Mr. Tipton bringing up the rear, they walked back up the winding trail to the new black Pontiac, the car Joe had bought with money earned for his part in helping win the 1948 World Series. Quickly his identity was proven, and kinder, more civil words were exchanged.

"Who's your folks, Joe Tipton?"

"My dad's name is Burt. Most people just called him 'Tip'."

"No sir, I don't recollect no Burt Tipton."

"Daddy works over there at that Copper Mine in Copperhill, Tennessee. Married my mom, Nolie Lou. She was a Leatherwood, part Cherokee, from down there at Cherry Log. I got four brothers and two sisters. Maybe you knew my Uncle Gordon? He once lived up here near High Dial, Georgia."

"Yes sir. I did hear tell of him, but I don't recollect ever making his acquaintance."

Mr. Tipton's composure suddenly changed again. Defeat and dejection settled on the big man. He bowed his head and muttered, "I'm truly sorry for the way I acted." He stopped speaking and appeared to be wrestling with a decision. Finally, he said, "Joe, would you mind going with me over to my house? There's something I want to show you. Maybe you'll see why I acted the way I did, if you go home with me."

Joe gladly agreed. Together they traveled together up a pig trail of a road in Joe's new Pontiac, to an old cabin that was Mr. Tipton's humble mountain abode. On the trip, Mr. Tipton was silent, his gaze riveted on the Indian chief's head that was the car's fancy hood ornament.

"Get out and come on in the house," he said, as Joe parked the car in a packed-dirt clearing.

Mr. Tipton climbed a flint rock set of steps to the front porch, shot-gun broken down and slung at his side. Slowly and subdued, Joe followed in tow.

"Maw, I've got us some company," he announced. "He's another Tipton. Maybe even kinfolks, too."

"How do you do, Mrs. Tipton, Joe said, removing his ball cap and holding it over his chest."

She nodded, but quickly cut her clouded eyes at the floor.

Trying not to stare, but failing miserably, Joe's gaze was drawn to a young girl who sat silently in a wooden chair nearby, staring at nothing in particular. With a face void of expression, exhibiting nothing more than dull indifference, she held a beady-eyed doll in her open hands. Emptiness owned her, and she appeared traumatized, oblivious to her surroundings. The only sound she made was an occasional sniffle.

Tears returning, the big man uttered the unthinkable, in words broken by rage and grief. "You see what that bastard did to my little girl, Joe. He...he raped her this morning! And when I find him, I'm gonna kill him where he stands, or my name ain't Tipton!"

Looking closer, Joe grimaced, then flinched at the awful sight. Never had he seen such horror written on the face of one so young. She couldn't have been more than twelve. Not knowing quite how to respond, he asked Mr. Tipton to step back out onto the front porch. Privacy assured, Joe advised him that the law should be brought in to help. He promised to send the sheriff, who would find the rapist. That's his job, he told the heartbroken father. Rubbing away tears, Mr. Tipton agreed, and apologized again for the earlier confrontation.

A court hearing was held in the spring of 1949, the same spring Joe switched ball teams. He now played for the Chicago White Socks, and spring training was cut short for Joe because he had been subpoenaed for the hearing. All Joe's newly discovered relatives were in court that day, to hear him testify about what he saw the day he'd trespassed while quail hunting.

Mountain justice was swift and lived up to its reputation. Mr. Tipton had killed the rapist where he stood, just as he had vowed he would. The judge sent him to prison. Joe never saw Mr. Tipton again.

Joe Tipton, catcher for the Cleveland Indians in 1948.

It's a lovely lie,
"Lightning never strikes twice
in the same place."

 # LIGHTNING

It's a lovely lie, "Lightning never strikes twice in the same place." Scientific theory and volumes of solid research supported by empirical data suggest otherwise, but the myth persists. A triple tragedy for two families refuted this long cherished myth on the dairy farm where I was raised near McCaysville, Georgia.

A dairy provided a great opportunity to capitalize on our farm's natural assets. After World War II ended, many farms of North Georgia existed on this seemingly risk-free venture. Having a plentiful supply of land, water, and laborers, the essential resources for a dairy were there. Farm families were already accustomed to long, hard work days, and the transition from farming to a dairy operation was a natural. The economic climate was perfect for business growth as well. Demand for milk, butter and other dairy products grew after the war. Returning soldiers brought the demand. They had an appetite for modern conveniences and products. People wanted these products delivered to their home, and made available in neighborhood grocery stores, and our dairy met their demand.

Our dairy in the beginning was like the other dozen or so dairies in Fannin County. We had less than one hundred head of milk cows. Nine children in our family provided the labor, but additional laborers were still needed to operate the farm and move the milk to market. The Roy Dean family lived in a house on our farm and supplied this extra labor.

The Dean family was typical of many poor working families of North Georgia. The family had gone without many things during the war, and knew well the burden of farm life. Roy Dean's family of nine children grew their own food, drew water from a mountain spring, and had no electricity in their home. They cooked their food and boiled water to wash their clothes on a wood stove. All but the youngest of the Dean family worked in the dairy or in the corn and hay fields.

Arnold was the youngest of the Dean family. He and I were near the same age. At age four, neither of us could speak clearly. Arnold called me "Doe." I called him "R-mull." We were best of friends and not old enough to help with the seven-day-a-week farm or dairy duties. We both were nurtured by nature's lessons. Summer days we'd catch spring lizards, chase June bugs, or shoot marbles. Summer nights we'd play hoopy hide and catch lightning bugs, put them in mason jars, and set the jars by our beds. In the winter we'd play Cowboys and Indians or play in the hayloft where we'd construct tunnels, caves, and secret hideouts.

The horrible reality and power of lightning was made known to R-mull and me one hot summer afternoon. His dad was driving up the cows from the lower bottom for their evening milking. Barefooted, R-mull and I joined his dad, where we dodged pasture patties and horse needle briars, and picked at daisies along the way. Like many farm-oriented people, Mr. Dean was proud, independent, and refused milk from the dairy. Instead, he owned his own milk cow that shared the pasture with the dairy herd. The Dean cow trailed far behind the herd on this frightful day.

A bolt of lightning struck far behind us and the main herd. Our hair stood up and the cracking sound stung our ears. Then we heard the rumble, and felt the rushing of wind. The cows were terrified and we watched them bee-line for the barn ahead, seeking shelter. Mr. Dean glanced back to see if his cow still followed. She had been struck by the lightning. We all ran back to where she lay almost motionless on the ground. Her tongue hung out, her moans were chaotic, and her glazed eyes glared as she made sporadic stiff-legged kicks. Then she died. Mr. Dean couldn't believe what we all saw happen. With a look of shock, desperation and defiance, he looked up into the black clouds and cried, "Why me Lord? Why my cow? Out of all these here cows, why'd ye take my cow?"

Sideways rain pelted us as we stared at the dead

cow. Then we all ran to the milk barn, where the herd was hunkered up close together, anxious, waiting to be milked and fed their evening meal of silage. At the milk barn, my older brother Gene tried to console Mr. Dean, and told him he'd get the tractor and help him bury the cow after the storm blew over. Mr. Dean didn't respond.

Lightning struck again the following summer. The strike wasn't seen, but the evidence was clear. The middle barn of our three barns burned to the ground. The strike had hit only a few hundred feet from the site of the earlier, lethal strike that killed the Dean family's milk cow. Insurance investigators ruled that the barn didn't take a direct hit. Instead, an induced strike had ignited the fresh hay stored in the barn's loft, and sparked spontaneous combustion.

Afterwards, the burned barn was built back, and the dairy business was good for a few years. Then times turned hard. A living could no longer be made. The economy was bad and too many farmers turned dairy men had created a glut of milk in North Georgia.

The Crawford Dairy had modernized during the few good years. Automatic milking machines, pasteurizers, chillers, and homogenizers were housed in a new block farm building, where over one hundred cows were milked twice daily. My brother Gene once injured his tongue in a bet about the modern equipment. He was offered a quarter if he would touch his tongue to the milk chiller. Gene won the bet, but lost a layer of skin from his tongue. The freezing cold metal glued his tongue to the giant tank. A little warm water got him unstuck.

The third strike of lightning again hit near the site of the cow killing and the middle barn burning. This time it hit the main milk barn. Everything was lost; all the modern machines and equipment were destroyed, and the Crawford Dairy suffered great financial loss. With no means to milk the cows, and the milk market being depressed, my dad made a decision to sell all the milk cows and get out of the dairy business. Our family returned to farming only, but on a much smaller scale.

Grim misfortune tragically struck down the Dean family near this same time. R-mull's mother died from an aggressive form of cancer. Mr. Dean was devastated. He fought a losing battle against the bottle. The children were soon taken away. R-mull and his siblings were raised in the Georgia Baptist Childrens Home near Macon, Georgia. My dad drove them there in the fall of 1959. That was the last time I ever saw R-mull.

She was a Tennessee cow and, truth be known, I reckon I was partly to blame for bringing that old blue nose heifer with the white star on her forehead into Georgia.

MILKLESS

"**I**mpossible!"

To sum it all up in one word, that's what the man said. Then he explained why, although I knew what I'd seen. "A cow is not capable, either anatomically or physiologically, of withdrawing milk from its own udders." He spit out the words almost as if he thought we were total idiots.

In the summer of sixty-one, that's what that new veterinarian, Joe Williams, from over in Coletown, Tennessee, had told my Daddy. "A milk cow simply can't milk itself," he'd insisted. Still, I knew I hadn't imagined it. That long, pitch-black limousine of a heifer with the white star in her forehead, had contorted her body and, just like a newborn calf, had started nursing from her own udders.

When I told my older and best buddy, T-Bone Watkins, he believed me. T-Bone told me he'd once paid a quarter to see a four-horned goat at the Blue Ridge Fair. He'd also paid another quarter to see a chicken play a piano. T-Bone and I were both friends of a dog with three legs, but that really wasn't much pumpkin. You see, it was Jerry Baker's dog. Old Three-foot liked to chase cars. One day that mutt captured a GMC pickup, but got stuck and dragged between the running board and terra firma. Jerry's poor pup lost a limb due to his passionate pursuit and subsequent apprehension of that pickup.

Daddy was less sanguine about the missing milk. He was in fact, conflicted, mad, and as ill as a hornet. I thought he was going to jump all over me, but he didn't. The conundrum upset him and the mystery amused him none what-so-ever. He didn't know whose word to take. He didn't want to believe that high-dollar cow college doctor from Tennessee, but he also doubted what a highly imaginative twelve year-old kid might or might not have seen. He cogitated the matter and came up with a hypothesis.

His theory was that "a stray rogue calf was probably stealing the cow's milk." He offered as visual, physical evidence the cow's red and raw tits. "That cow's udder would be 'bagging up' if she was holding up her milk," he argued. Still, Daddy had his doubts. Where was the missing milk going, he wondered? Adequate evidence was lacking. An experiment to find the truth behind the mystery was ordered, and I was appointed executor.

To solve the mystery, Daddy used scientific methodology. He told me to "pen her up by herself so no rogue calf can get to her milk. Watch that cow with every spare minute you have." His experiment proved nothing. The sequestered cow still gave no milk, her udders did not expand, and her tits were still red and raw. Even stranger, she ate little hay or crushed corn and was growing fat. Everyone was confused and confounded. All any of us knew with certainty was that an eight-hundred pound milk cow was not giving us enough milk to keep a cat alive. But from whence came this enigmatic, 'divine-bovine' possessing Harry Houdini skills?

She was a Tennessee cow and, truth be known, I reckon I was partly to blame for bringing that old blue nose heifer with the white star on her forehead into Georgia. Two weeks before, a man in Pine Ridge, Tennessee, by the name of Eschol Wishon, had sent word to Daddy that he was "in the market" for a new milk cow. He had a cow to trade in on a new one. We didn't have a new milk cow to trade him, but having raised veal calves before, and having just traded for a worthless, suck-egg dog, I hatched an idea. I was sneaky proud of this plan. It would make me some quick money. My plan would also bring justice to the "done wrong" dog deal, and assuage the grievances I'd suffered from that deal. This ploy was as right as rain in a drought. Well, maybe so. Only time would tell.

The game plan was that we'd pen up a little

muley, mongrel cow we had that resembled Elsie, of Borden's Dairy TV fame. She was already going dry for the summer, so we wouldn't milk her. That way her udders would swell up, and she'd look like a fresh milk cow that had just "come in" with a new baby calf. We'd go to the Murphy Stock barn, where I'd gotten that suck-egg dog, and buy her an adopted baby calf. One could be bought for less than a dollar; sometimes dairy farmers would even give them away for free, especially if the newborn calf had the scours and was expected to die. I elected to pay fifty cents for a healthy calf, and the adoption was completed. The new calf received no milk from her new mama at first, so we nursed the calf with a bottle for a few days instead.

After about a week, we loaded "Elsie" and her newly adopted baby onto our farm truck. Off to Pine Ridge we went to trade cows, and hopefully get "boot" in the trade. First we tied shut the calf's jaws to prevent it from sucking Elsie's bulging udders. Just before we arrived at Mr. Wishon's residence, we would untie the calf's jaw, and allow them to "bond" like a regular mama cow and her calf would naturally connect.

The road trip over to the customer's house was fun. Pine Ridge was located just beyond Harbuck, Tennessee, just past the L&N Railroad Crossing. Few houses could be seen on the paved road part of the trip.

More copious for our viewing pleasure were several neon-adorned beer joints. Equally prevalent were Holiness Churches. Finally, more houses were glimpsed on the graveled road part of the trip. Also, belly-high fields of corn nearing completed cultivation and subsequent laying-by, were in evidence.

We passed a brush arbor where church was being held daily during the hottest part of the day, under the shade of a leaf covered shed. A farmer plowed a bay mule on a distant emerald green hill, and with a sweep plow, he cultivated dense green stalks of corn. There, in front of the brush arbor, Daddy stopped the truck and I removed the tie-strings and un-muzzled the jaws of Elsie's adopted calf. Then we journeyed on to Mr. Wishon's humble abode.

Across the road from an old lean-to looking shanty of a house babbled a swift running creek. Atop the creek, standing prominent and proud, was an outhouse. All deposits made from the outhouse freely floated away, down the creek, guided by gravity and God, buoyed and bound for places unknown. Foundation logs traversed the creek and supported the outhouse. An exquisite quarter-moon cutout graced the privy's entry door.

Daddy had told me, "Now, let me do most of the talking unless I ask you something during the trading talk." He'd parked the truck and had immediately started a casual conversation with Mr. Wishon.

In the back of the farm truck, Wishon witnessed the newly adopted calf going to town on Elsie's sore and utterly overfull udders with gusts of glory and hungry resolve. Mama cow freely acquiesced; Elsie's discomfort from storing a week's worth of milk was being relieved. Daddy read Mr. Wishon's look of excitement over the new cow and baby calf. Cow-trading talk commenced.

"Well, I'd have to have your cow and a hundred dollars boot money for us to trade cows," my Daddy offered. A quick declining counter-quip shot back, "Carl, I ain't got that kind of money. I just got through building a brand new house." He pointed up toward the top of a small rocky knoll, where red mud seemed to ooze and dribble down. On this red mud clearing stood a shotgun, paint-bare house. The roofline had a serious sag in it, and made me think of that old swayback mare Daddy had bought from Chester Wombel the week before.

Wishon's negotiating continued, sprinkled liberally with words of woe. "You won't probably believe it, but that house up yonder costed me over three hundred dollars to build for my family. But drought-take-it, I got to have a milk cow for my children. They'uns get rickets iffen they don't get milk to drank." He said this while looking down at a snaggle-tooth girl with bare feet, who held her squirming baby sister on her hip. "Could you afford to take fifty dollars boot?"

Daddy cut his eyes at me and asked, "What do you think, Joe?"

I said, "Would you consider splitting the difference Mr. Wishon? Give us seventy-five dollars and your cow, and we'll trade?"

Dad interjected, "Mr. Wishon, you're getting two cows with this deal. We're only getting one cow. That little heifer calf there will grow up to make you another milk cow."

"All right, I'll do it! We'll trade. I'll give you seventy-five dollars boot. You can unload them over there at that road bank. I'll put a halter on old Blue Bell and bring her on over to your truck". He said this, while pointing toward a barn that looked more structurally stable than his newly-built, sway-back mansion on the hill.

We exchanged cows and money. Everyone smiled and shook hands, then we drove the farm truck back to the brush arbor. Daddy never saw a church meeting he didn't like, and this one was no exception. He and I took a seat on a pine slab bench beside a smirking, big heavy woman, who held a Bruton's snuff can in one hand, and a can of spit in the other. Beside her sat a young, skinny girl with stringy, burnt brown hair. On her knee she bounced a disgruntled baby with two teeth. Together, we all waited patiently for the preacher. A full bucket of well water sat near a makeshift pulpit up front, that had also been built from pine slabs.

The day was African hot and sticky. The shade of the arbor availed little relief, and everyone was fanning with their funeral home fans. After being breastfed, the baby relented from its restlessness and napped. Beads of condensation streamed down the cold, steel, water bucket, then splattered onto the fresh-sawn sawdust floor.

The sound of jingling trace chains broke the silence and slowly grew louder. Then the man we had seen earlier cultivating the corn field meandered toward the arbor. Chains stopped jingling. The harnessed mule he led was hitched to a fence post and given a stalk of corn to munch on. The man ducked under the arbor's rear entry, sauntered on over, and removed the dipper from the water bucket. He ladled up a dipper full and gulped it down, spilling some on his chin and bib overalls. Wiping water from his chin and neck, and sweat from his brow with a red bandana, then he thumbed through a tiny Holy Bible he'd removed from the center pocket of his overalls, and said, "First thang, let's make a joyful noise to the Lord afore I commence to preach 'The Word'." With wooden puppet-like motions, he led the sparse congregation in two verses of an a cappella "Amazing Grace", then read some scripture from Revelation. Between the sucking air sounds of a Kentucky Derby racehorse fighting for air, he proceeded to deliver rants and raves about the iniquity and deception amongst people and their modern churches. His recurring message was, "We's living in the 'End Times' I tell ya. It's time for you people to get right with God."

The message made me feel contrite about the cow trade transaction I'd just conducted, but I repented of nothing. After what seemed like three days of hearing "The Word," drowsy silence settled in. The napping baby awoke and began to stir and whine. The tone of the breath-deprived preacher changed. His face was as red as a pickled beet, and he sounded exhausted, but still he was obviously well pleased with his sermon. The tired preacher, who had finally slowed to a wheezy talk, eased over to the water bucket and gulped down another dipper of water, wiping sweat at the same time. He pocketed the red bandana and gave a call for all sinners to come to the pine slab altar to pray for forgiveness of their sins. Mercifully, the services soon ended.

An imminent and angry thunder cloud now hung over the brush arbor. In the distance lightning cracks and thunder rolling hinted at what was to come. Fearfully, for a split-second, I fretted and wondered if maybe he'd been right about The End Times being near. This farmer cum preacher and prophet ignored the rumbling and moseyed over to the mule and unhitched her. Once again, the trace chains jingled, and he hummed a hymn as he led the mule up the trail, back to the emerald hillside corn field. Daddy and I dashed for the farm truck like two scared lizards. We rode away, taking Blue Bell to her new home in Georgia.

In about a week's time, a phone call came and a message was left for Daddy. The caller was Mr. Eschol Wishon and he had his dander up. Mama gave Daddy the message. "Tell your husband I wish he'd come and get this 'fresh calf and gone-dry cow' of his'n. Tell him to bring me back my seventy-five dollars and old Blue Bell. At least old Bell give nearly enough milk to feed hern self."

Mr. Wishon got his wish the very next day.

Foreman Frank Ray kept his eyes on the road and said nothing during the flare-up. He'd heard plenty of quarrels over card game money before. Not being able to calculate money change was usually the cause of the disputes.

# POKER

Chicken catchers from the tri-state Georgia, Tennessee, and North Carolina area were a different breed of people. They were almost a cult unto themselves and, like birds of a feather, they flocked together. They freely accepted their fate in life and their life's goal was simple: Survive. A chicken catcher did not question why he'd been dropped into a universe he didn't understand, or why he'd been poorly equipped to deal with that universe over which he had no control. He also had no dreams of being assimilated into "normal" society, but felt strongly, he had as much right to "be there and breathe air" as anyone else. I don't recall ever knowing a chicken catcher who was "depressed," or who acted sophisticated.

Most catchers were school drop outs. In some cases, they couldn't even write their own names or make money change. As students, they hadn't sat at the front of the class; they hadn't played "rock, paper, scissors" at recess. Instead, they were the students at the back of the class; the ones who'd swap shoulder slugs and bet cigarettes on the winner of this game of "give and take." They played the game until school was out for them – usually well before the eighth grade.

The chicken catchers believed in three principles. One: Hard work was theirs. Two: An economic system existed, but they weren't part of it. Three: Luck rather than work was their most likely ticket to a better life. Guided by these principles the chicken catcher battled in his strange universe.

From the age of eleven to age seventeen, I worked at night with these chicken catchers. This story recalls some of the calamities faced by my chicken catcher buddies.

The chickens to be caught were located nine miles from nowhere in a little mountain community called Shoal Creek, North Carolina. A creek, shoal or otherwise, was nowhere to be seen on this late January winter night in 1964 – when Mother Nature and mischievous human behavior created mayhem in the mountains.

The chicken catchers were transported in an old Dodge panel truck (The Crate) owned by The Poetry Company. The owner's actual name was Crawford "Poultry" Company, but we catchers liked and used the other mispronounced name better. In route to Shoal Creek, The Crate would turn right off of Highway 64 near The Miami Café in Murphy and follow a road along the Hiawassee River. Then, a sharp right was taken. Up a narrow curving gravel road led to a feather nest filled with chickens. Through a deep hollow and then up a series of pine sheltered mountains the old panel truck fought its way to the feather nests. Eighty-five hundred White Rock, heavy hens would be caught and loaded onto three chicken trucks before sunup. Or so we thought.

The chicken catchers were a rough and rowdy bunch. They had a restless nature and constantly ribbed, bantered, and pestered each other – even when they were sober and not in jail. Tonight their restless behavior was even more lively than usual. The unsettled, failing weather made them nervous and more jumpy than usual.

The sky was a steely gray. The mercury had shrunk and sunk to the bottom of the Co' Cola thermostat that hung outside the entryway to The Poetry Company office. The wind was damp and biting, and brought an unexpected misery to the cold. That white (greasy skid stuff) might precipitate at any time, but weather never stopped chickens from being caught and loaded. Neither rain, sleet, snow, or gloom of night could keep the crew of The Crate from their work. No chickens caught meant no money made. The mantra of the chicken catchers was: "Come Hell or High Water, The Feather Necks Must Ride".

Snowy weather had just the opposite effect on chickens. They became more passive. The sting on a cold hand caused by a flogging hen was less likely to occur. They pecked the catchers less, and they put up little fight when being caught in snowy weather. Hens were silent and docile when a hint of snow was present. That was a good thing, because patience was not a common virtue found in those chicken catchers. Often, an ill natured rooster or an old setting hen lost its life before even leaving the feather nest, if they made the mistake of flogging the wrong chicken catcher.

Tonight, the old smoke-filled Crate was crammed. It indeed looked worthy of its nickname, stuffed like an over-full chicken crate with too many catchers. Frank Ray was the foreman and driver. He was a bit high strung. Tonight a Russian fur hat covered Frank's balding head. Beside him, seated in the coveted up-front shotgun seat, was W.B. Ray.

W.B. was a senior catcher. He was a man's man, resolute and of large frame. A match stick always dangled from W.B.'s lip. Tonight, a black toboggan gathered and shrouded W.B.'s kinky Brillo® pad hair; he wore his trademark green army surplus coat, and a three day beard dusted his leathery face. The coat usually stayed unzipped, no matter the weather. W.B. had a speech impediment – many of his words were pronounced with a "sh" prefix. W.B. called the foreman "Shrank" instead of Frank. Frank took no offense with his cousin's unique pronunciation.

Two younger catchers were seated behind "Shrank" and W.B. on opposite facing benches. Up close and in each other's face, they breathed the other's breath. Passionately, they argued about something they each valued dearly, something equating currency among the catchers – cigarettes.

"Give me a drag off that duck of yourn, cowboy! I'll pay ye back on payday."

"Buy yor own damn cigarettes! I do. I ain't yah Mama and I didn't take you to raise!"

"Well! If 'at's the way you're going to be about it, then fine. I won't ast your stingy ass for another damn thang for as long as I'm kicking. Wait'll you need a smoke and I got 'em and you hain't. See what happens then."

"Suits the hell out of me! You damn tick."

Winking one eye, he then handed the entreating catcher a fresh "Pell Mall." A match box rattled. A scratched match flashed a flame, playing light off the shadowy faces of other catchers lining the inside of the dimly lit old panel truck. Looking away, he ignored the lit match he'd centered over the chicken coop bottom and makeshift poker table. Cupped hands protected the flame as the pleader leaned in and lit his borrowed cigarette. Sucking a puff, he leaned back, and promised, "I'll pay ye back, soon as I get my rich uncle out'n The Poor House."

"Yeah, yeah, yeah. Like hell you will. That's what ye told me the last time; you damn blood sucker."

The red hot poker game continued as though no words had been exchanged. A premonition of foreboding filled the cold, dank air. All the catchers knew a rough night lay ahead, but they didn't talk about it. Instead, they concentrated on the poker game. The oppressive cold had stirred a different batch of emotions. Riding together and watching the poker game somehow diverted and relieved their anxiety. In the cold, smoke-filled Crate, they sensed unity and safety; together, they were a part of something bigger than themselves.

Back in the corner of The Crate sat a catcher who was a little too quiet. Bill Carter was a twenty-something age man from Turtletown, Tennessee, and he had been out of the pen for only a few days. Serving time wasn't unusual for chicken catchers. It was also common for the foreman to have to bail the catchers out of jail. Bill was a small man, and he wore a new hat with dog-ear flaps. In one hand he held a knife and in the other, a sharpening stone. Bill spoke to no one. Aloof by choice, he sat and sharpened his knife. His face and eyes told us he knew something that we didn't.

Next to Bill sat Ed Cross, a rotund, red apple-faced man with sensitive, searching eyes. Ed wore bib overalls and a train engineer's cap. I knew Ed. He had plowed cornfields with a mule one summer for my dad. Brother Jim and I hoed Johnson grass from the same rows he plowed. Ed had been paid fifty cents an hour, and I was greatly impressed one week, when Dad gave Ed a check for forty dollars for plowing that mule.

I also remember the day Ed's mama passed away. It was morning and the fog had just burned off the meadow down on Mill Creek, the meadow we called "The Lower Bottom." On that midsummer morning, Ed's mule pulled a cultivator sweep plow; it was hot and humid, and near corn "laying-by time". Dad gave Ed the sad news. He walked to the edge of the field and waited for Ed and the mule to get to his end of the row. In the searing sun, Ed squalled like a baby as he led the mule from the corn field.

Sometimes I still see images of Ed, with his shoulders jerking up and down; his faded bib overalls following those bouncing shoulders; the calloused hands that uncoupled the trace chains, and held the reins of that dumb mule – the one that indifferently nipped at corn stalks – as Ed cried out to God in humble hurt.

With the expression of a fly swatter on his face, seated directly across from Ed, was a young, slender built guy. He had a big nose and lots of bones in his face and his skinny neck looked like a chicken's leg. His name was Glover Parr and a flattened-down taxi cab driver's hat crowned his pointy head. Through green teeth, he hesitantly puffed on a Prince Albert rolled smoke. Squint-eyed, he let the cigarette hang and smolder. Glover rarely spoke unless spoken to. His speech was slow, and not much seemed to be going on under that short-billed flat hat he wore. His words were always measured, as though they were destined to be frozen for eternity in blocks of ice. Glover was a steady chicken catcher, but his pace, like his speech, was extra slow.

As The Crate rolled toward Shoal Creek, two catchers folded their cards and dropped out of the poker game.

"Get me to hell out of this game!" one protested, and slammed down his folded cards on the coop bottom.

Two new players entered the game and took their places. Both new catchers had been picked up at Clont's Store in Isabella, Tennessee, making five catchers total in the game that night. Each pitched a nickel ante toward the pot, located in the middle of the coop bottom. A new hand of five card stud was dealt; two cards fell: one face up and one face down.

Often accounting accuracy was dubious where the pot money was concerned, and was a point of contentious debates. This was the case tonight.

"All Right, Greenhorn, you've got the high card with 'at air King I dealt ye. How much you gonna bet on it?"

"I got a nickel right cher I'm gonna bet." He then pitched another nickel to the pot. All players except one called the bet. Then, the last player threw in a fifty cent piece and, at the same time slid all other coins away from the pot. Instantly a quarrel about the money in the pot ensued:

"Hey pecker-head, you owe the pot money! I'd pre-chate it if you'd make the pot right. You can't just rake everything out of the pot like 'at, cause you done put 'at BIG MONEY in 'ere."

"Well, no I don't owe the pot nary a thang. See, I put in a fifty cent piece. Mr. Clonts over at Clont's Store done told me it was the same as having ten Buffalo nickels. Uh, don't ye see right tare, they's same as ten nickels in the pot now."

"You and that man in Isabella, Tennessee are both fuller of shit than a Christmas Turkey," came the chastising rebuff from the dealer. "If you' gonna play in this here game, you need to put some more money in the pot!"

"I did! I put fifty cents," the accused protested in an even louder voice. "How much is it you're a reckoning I owe the pot!" he snapped.

"Well, hell, I don't know, but you need to put something else in 'at pot 'sides that big-ass coin. Maybe two nickels'll do. Yeah, 'at sounds 'bout right to me. Two more nickels."

Two of the other players, the ones not from Isabella, emphatically and wholeheartedly concurred. Two nickels from the protesting player would make the pot right, they reasoned.

"Look guys, I hain't puttin' nary another damn penny in 'at pot! The pot, right tare, it's right!" he bristled, pointing toward the center of the coop bottom. "They aught ta be fifty cents in that pot and By-God, 'at's what's in 'ere! That fifty cent piece is the same as ten nickels. Mr. Clonts told me so."

"I ain't dealing nary another card 'til you make the pot right," the dealer declared.

"Well to hell with all of you'ins, then. I'll not play. I'll just put these here nickels back in the pot and ketchaholt of my fifty cent piece," he stormed. "You'ins can all just go to hell and play by you'ins self."

"That'll be just fine! If you're going to try to shit us out of our money, then we don't want you in our poker game."

"Fine! Deal me out!" he howled. Coins scrapped over a flat surface – nine nickels screeched across a wooden coop bottom - his shaky hand shoved all the nickels into the pot. His other nervy hand snatched up the prominent fifty cent piece. The BIG MONEY was his again.

The banned player clutched the half-dollar between his thumb and index finger. He fidgeted with the coin. Nervously he twirled the coin, and would rub its rough edge as though it was a magic genie bottle filled with wishes.

Foreman Frank Ray kept his eyes on the road and said nothing during the flare-up. He'd heard plenty of quarrels over card game money before. Not being able to calculate money change was usually the cause of the disputes. When things got silent, Frank inconspicuously stole a glance to read the faces of the chicken catchers, just to make certain no fight was brewing. The Crate rambled on up Bell Hill Straight, toward North Carolina.

As they left Tennessee and crossed the North

Carolina line, Glover Parr glared, eye-ball to eye-ball, at Ed Cross. Peering and turning his head like a chicken hawk, he then droned slow and slanderous words to the other catchers, "Did ya'll know that old Ed Cross here can't get no babies. He's a 'bar hog.' He can't make no lit' lens."

"Shut your damn mouth, Glover! You don't know what you're talking about," was the hasty protest from Ed who was caught off guard.

"Well, how many babies you got "BAR?" came Glover's drawn out drawl. "You been married a spell now, and you hain't got nary a baby yet?"

"God damn you, Glover! Don't you call me "BAR. If you call me BAR one more time, I'm ah, I'm ah, libel to cut ye," Ed threatened, faking a fast reach for his back pocket.

With the same poker face, Glover ground out a cold insensitive monotone quip. "Now…you…wouldn't…wanna…do…dat…now,…would…you…BAR?"

Ed shut his eyes and hung his head; not in shame or defeat, but in mindful pity for Glover, who continued to stare. Ed's engineer's cap now held his full attention. Silence screamed inside The Crate. The only sounds heard were poker cards being dealt. They swished in time to the rhythmic beat of the old Crate's six-pack muffler.

Riding now on North Carolina's new asphalt paved road, we were half way to Murphy. So far, no fights had started and no one had been cut, but the night was still young.

At the rear of the truck and across from Bill Carter sat the Tankersley twins, Carlie and Charlie. Both young men wore highly-shined combat boots. Nothing covered their immaculately groomed jet-black hair. Carlie sat directly opposite Bill Carter. Between them, rested The Crate's spare tire. Carlie proudly rested one shiny boot atop that tire.

Without warning, a maniacal smile creased Carter's face. Lunging forward, he rested the knife's edge on the toe of Carlie's boot, then laughed like a mad man, and asked, "I wonder if my knife is sharp enough yet."

The smile left as quickly as it had come, and he pressed down on the knife handle. Carlie quickly jerked his foot away, but wasn't quite fast enough. The toe of the boot now lay wide open and a white sock was exposed. Threads stuck out, silhouetted against the gleaming black boot. Carlie's shoe and sock had been cut, but miraculously, his foot wasn't.

"Look what you've done, you damn crazy bastard! You've ruined my boot! Put that damn knife up unless you plan on using it."

Carter remained mute. Again he displayed the smile of one who has escaped from a mental institution. Then he started sharpening his knife again, slow and methodical like. Things got funeral home quiet again. Frank looked back to see what was up, but saw nothing. Everyone was looking down at each others' shoes.

Before The Crate reached The Miami Café in Murphy, Carter got that crazy smile on his face once again. He looked at Carlie. This time, however, he arose from his seat and placed the knife's edge on Carlie's forearm, near the elbow. Carlie flinched, and this time the razor-sharp edge severed Carlie's red and black flannel shirt, and the gray sweat-shirt he wore underneath.

Carlie raised his arm, scanned the damaged garment, and shouted with a clear mixture of disbelief, anger, and horror in his voice:

"Are you crazy, man? Now look what you've done to my shirt!"

Carter, with dog-ears and the price tag flapping around his new hat, said nothing. Instead, he turned and glared at Carlie, smirked, and began a series of rapid-fire braying laughs.

The knife had cut clean; no frays or hanging threads this time. A thin, four-inch slit lined the forearm of Carlie's flannel shirt, and at first, he didn't realize he was bleeding. We didn't see the blood either. The smoke and dingy light in the rear of The Crate blurred our vision. When Carlie finally realized his arm had been sliced open, he tearfully told Carter, "You put that damn knife up or use it, one or tother!"

Frank's sixth sense and experience told him something was going on in the back. He pulled over at The Miami Café and gave Carter an order, "Get the fuck out. You damn drunk, crazy bastard. If you're gonna work for The Poetry Company, you gonna hafta stay sober. You can wait here at the Miami. If you put away that knife and sober up, we might let you ride home with us when we come back in the morning, but you ain't working with us tonight. Now get the hell out."

Carter accepted the order without protest. For the first time, he looked conscious and alert. He closed the knife with a click, and pocketed it and the sharpening stone. Then he stumbled from The Crate. All other catchers except Carlie and Charlie also left the truck. They all walked quietly toward the entrance of The Miami Café, keeping their distance from Carter, who walked the deliberate, concentrated, but limber leg walk of a drunk. With Frank listening, Charlie demanded without trying to hide his anger, "Carlie, you want me to go stomp a mud-hole in that guy with the knife? That crazy son of a bitch!"

"No! Hell, no! I kin fight my own damn fights. Don't need nobody to help me," was Carlie's combative response, spoken through quivering lips nonetheless.

Frank quickly interrupted the debate with an order. "You ain't going nowhere, Charlie! Now, sit your ass down. You stay right here with your brother. We've got to take him to the hospital and get that arm sewed up. Wait here. I'll tell the guys in the Café we're going, but we'll be back."

With the twins as his only passengers, Frank pulled away from The Miami, and sped to the hospital. Giant flakes of snow swirled in the dim evening light, as the three exited The Crate and jetted towards the emergency room entrance. Charlie stayed with his brother during the procedure.

Frank returned to The Miami, picked up the other catchers, all except Bill Carter, and drove them on to the feather nest in Shoal Creek. Later, he returned to the hospital, picked up the twins, and brought them to the chicken house, where one truck was being loaded and another one waited to be loaded with White Rock heavy hens. The twins worked as though nothing had ever happened. Carlie, with only one good arm caught, but couldn't carry the heavy hens to the truck outside. The other catchers got a grip on Carlie's chickens and they carried his chickens for him to the truck. Helping others who were down on their luck was an unspoken code of the chicken catchers.

Frigid temps, snow or any kind of severe weather never seemed to lessen a chicken catcher's love for a powerful prank. A new catcher – a "greenhorn" – was usually the victim of those pranks. Tonight was no different.

 # DISPLACED

This night of chicken catching had started wrong and had gotten "wronger." Even the weather seemed to be headed south. At Shoal Creek, the wind stopped its blustery whistles and blasts. Between the mountains surrounding the feather nest, the wind was replaced by bitter cold. Damp, frigid air settled in, and the hard freeze brought with it a feeling of isolation and abandonment, but we weren't alone. Our breath, which we now could literally see, was our constant shadow.

Charlie and Carlie Tankersley had made it to Shoal Creek late, and were working to make up for lost time. Carlie, with only one good arm, thanks to another vindictive catcher's knife blade, could catch but couldn't carry the heavy hens all the way to the truck outside. Other catchers accepted Carlie's chickens, which they carried to the truck for him.

Cigarettes and chicken-catchers went together like ham and eggs. Just look for a hazy, dense cloud of smoke and inside it, you'd find a chicken catcher. Even in a dark chicken house, a red glowing dot in the midst of a foggy cloud of smoke always pinpointed their location. Tonight, it appeared that all the catchers were smoking. The true smokers, however, upon second glance, looked as though they were being led out and guided by their cigarettes. With hands full of chickens, determined catchers marched through the dark, balancing an extended red dot in one corner, and exhaling smoke and fog out the other corner of their mouths.

As the crew worked, walls of filled and stacked chicken coops steadily climbed. The cold air, somehow, made even the wooden chicken coops feel lighter than an egg shell. Every chicken catcher was hyperactive, as though they'd taken a hand full of uppers or bennies. But they hadn't. They kept moving; even when they had no chickens to carry, they moved. It was one way to stay warm in those cold, North Carolina mountains.

Standing beside the engine of the chicken truck gave some relief from the bone-chilling cold. These gigantic truck engines rumbled and roared, radiating glorious warmth and a few toxic fumes. Truck drivers would never allow a catcher to sit in their warm truck cabs. A sleeping driver, laying across the truck seats, precluded entry. If you stood by an engine too long, a message would be sent via air mail in the form of an egg hurled at the catcher who stood slacking off. It didn't matter that you were cold. Everyone was cold.

It was well past midnight when I stood there,

accompanied only by my visible breath, alongside the engine of the loaded and parked chicken truck. I'd positioned myself, jogging in place, trying to get my feet warm. Other catchers busied themselves. Behind me, I heard their dialog. "Headache! Chain coming across, boss-man!"

"Let her rip cowboy!"

The next sound was a crisp crack of cold steel striking against frozen wood, followed by the rippling, jingling music of chains flying across the ricts. The chains were buckled down to hold the coops in place. Finally, they installed a tarp across the front ricts of coops. These were the assigned duties of the "truck workers" and not that of a catcher like me, whose responsibility was to catch and carry the chickens from the chicken house to the truck. Still, this fine distinction regarding the limits of my responsiblities was not fully understood or accepted by all my fellow catchers.

I was made painfully aware of this misunderstanding as I stood alongside the engine of an old I-190 International Harvester chicken truck. Suddenly I felt an intense burning in my lower left leg, followed by a throbbing ache. We'd fully loaded one truck without a foreman and three missing catchers. Quite a feat, I had proudly told myself. I'd done my job for now. So, why not warm myself and take a little break, I reasoned.

The pain made me think I'd been hit by a rock. At first, I thought the burn was the familiar sting caused by a hurled egg, but this was even more painful. Something was definitely different. An air mail message had been delivered. But, there was no splash. Also missing was the sticky goo that should have coated my pants. And there were no bits of chipped egg shell. So, what had hit me? Was it a falling star that had randomly landed, popping the knot on my leg that I was rubbing, now desperate for relief? I had to know.

I borrowed a flashlight from the truck driver. Aiming its beam of light around the frozen gravel where I had stood, I didn't see any local rocks or alien meteorites that looked out of place. At least none that looked like the one that might have bounced off my leg. Instead, what I found was an egg. A frozen egg! Great, I'd been hit by a no-splash egg while trying to stay warm. Still, the message had been sent and received: "Get back to work, slacker!"

Frigid temps, snow or any kind of severe weather never seemed to lessen a chicken catcher's love for a powerful prank. A new catcher – a "greenhorn" – was usually the victim of those pranks. Tonight was no different. On this oppressively cold night Pee Wee would be the victim. True to his name, he was small, but he was a gritty and willing team worker, eager to please the boss and gain acceptance of the crew. Tonight he wore a double-billed, front and back, Sherlock Holmes hat that he'd pulled way down on his head, so that it hid most of his face.

With the hat's ear flaps tied up over his head, one bemused catcher had told Pee Wee, "Hey, greenhorn! I can't tell if you're comin' or a goin' in that catch me/go-to-hell hat." Pee Wee humored him by flashing a missing tooth smile. Later, when the sun sank behind the mountains, the temperature dropped lower than Santa's drawers in a North Pole outhouse. Only then did Pee Wee finally untie and drop down the earflaps.

An inch of snow blanketed the ground as work began on loading the second truck from the second house, adjacent to and parallel with the first house. Except for the roosters, the first house had been totally emptied, and with its glaring overhead lights, the empty house now looked bigger. It felt colder, as well, now that it was missing the fat, warm hens.

Pee Wee was approached by a senior catcher carrying an order. Pee Wee was attempting to remove six hens from their roost. "Boss man told me to tell you, he wants you to catch nothing but the roosters; for you not to catch any hens. He wants you to catch these roosters right cher and carry them over to the house we just got done emptying. Put these roosters right cher, over there with the other roosters we left in that empty house."

Pee Wee was a street-wise teen. He had doubts and didn't immediately accept the order. Instead, he demanded, "We'll whyn't the boss come and tell me himself what it is he wants me to do? Why'd he send you?"

"Well, greenhorn," the messenger replied. "I tell ya, Foreman Frank's busy out there buckling down that first truck we just loaded. So, I'm the 'straw boss' and he told me to get word to you." Now you need to do what I'm telling you to do. Catch just the roosters. Carry them over there to that empty house and let'm go with the roosters we left over there. You got my meaning?"

"Yep, I see what you're saying. Don't make no sense to me, but if that's what the boss man wants, that's what the boss man gonna get."

Pee Wee worked harder than a rented mule at his new project. He went at it harder than a hungry hound on a bone. He first snatched a large rooster by one leg, pulling it from its roost. He tried to draw the rooster to his side, as he'd been taught to do with the hens. The rooster revolted violently, wanting no part of being captured. He flapped and flogged fiercely, using both wings, while he kicked and clawed with his single free leg. Then he pecked at his captor's leg, but the little guy held on to the defiant rooster. Pee Wee attempted to thrust the rooster away from his body in an effort to avoid the stinging wing swats. It appeared the rooster would fly away, carrying with it the small body of its would-be kidnapper. Then we heard Pee Wee exclaim, "Oh, damn! That hurt!" The rooster fell to the ground, gained its footing, and wobbled away into the dark.

Pee Wee instantly shook his hand trying to be certain it still worked. In the dark, hidden out of sight, the self-appointed straw boss sniggered silently, before he re-adjusted the grin he could barely contain. His straight face in place, he walked over to where Pee Wee stood nursing his injured hand. "Oh, forgot to tell you. Be careful what part of the leg you catch onto these roosters. They got some hellacious spurs on 'em."

Pee Wee said nothing but instead rubbed his wounded hand on his pant leg. He spat on his sore paw and snaked out his arm to catch another rooster. This time he caught both legs... above the spurs. Then he caught another.

One by one Pee Wee caught those roosters, which he wrestled into submission, then carried them from the full chicken house to the emptied number one house, now known to him as the "rooster house". When released, the displaced roosters ran like wild mustangs down the middle of their new, cold, and mostly empty surroundings.

As was the normal routine after loading a house of chickens, Foreman Frank walked from one end to the other end of the just emptied house. Mostly this was done to assure that all the hens had been caught, and loaded. As Frank entered the emptied house, he saw Pee Wee drop and release two roosters. Fury and bewilderment rolled over Frank and he hollered, "Hey you! Greenhorn! Come here!"

Pee Wee raced to where Frank stood. He was proud as a peacock of the more than fifty roosters he had personally relocated, and felt certain an "atta boy" was imminent. Frank scanned the house with all the roosters and then screamed at Pee Wee, "What...th'... hell... are you doing?"

Pee Wee felt like he'd been body-slammed, and pride was quickly replaced by shock and confusion. Frank's angry stance didn't make sense. The young man hesitated for a second before answering. Then, from under the bill of his Sherlock Holmes hat, came his sheepish response. "Well, the straw boss told me to catch all the roosters in house number two and put them in here with the other roosters. 'At's what I been doin'."

"Straw Boss? Straw... Boss! I don't got no straw boss. Have you lost your marbles?"

"Uh, no sir. I'm... uh...doing what I was told to do."

Frank scratched his head, then mumbled to himself, "I think I see what's going on here. Now you listen to me," he said to Pee Wee, "don't bring any more of them dang roosters into this house!" Looking sternly at the boy, Frank asked, "I guess you wouldn't want to tell me who this 'straw boss' feller is that put you up to moving these roosters, would you?"

Before Pee Wee could answer, a cacophony of flapping sounds interrupted, as a cloud of dust boiled up at the end of the chicken house. All the roosters appeared to be racing to a central location, and began attacking each other. Fights between several roosters broke out, where the visiting roosters were being assaulted by the resident roosters. With raisin-looking eyes peeping out from under his Sherlock Holmes hat, Pee Wee spied the rooster fights with unfettered glee. Another jack-o-lantern tooth smile raced to his face.

Pointing toward the rooster riot, Frank barked an order. "Hurry down yonder where that light switch is on the wall!" He pointed toward a location near the front of the house. "Throw it and turn out the lights! They'll stop fighting if we put 'em back in the dark."

Pee Wee sprang into action and sprinted toward the light switch, drop kicking any roosters that tried to impede his progress along the way. This made Frank even more furious, and he mumbled several colorfully-choice words as his hands flailed frantically above his head in frustration. Pee Wee, who had now distanced himself from Frank, was ignorant to the drama playing out behind him. As the lights went out, Foreman Frank spun around and stalked away.

Soon he returned to the darkened chicken house with another catcher. Deliberately shining a flashlight on Pee Wee's face, his voice was stern as he told the boy and the other catcher, "You fellers catch every dang one of these roosters! Carry them over to the other house. If we leave them here, without the hens to keep them peaceful, they're liable to kill each other. Switch the lights back on when you've got them all moved. The owner wants the lights left on in here. Maybe by morning they'll settle down and won't fight each other."

With his temper finally under control, Frank walked away, spitting and muttering to himself. "Good

Gawd! What else can go wrong tonight?"

In the cold, dark, mostly empty chicken house, Pee Wee and his assistant began catching and moving the warring roosters; even the ones that Pee Wee had just brought over were returned. Outside, in the roadway between the two chicken houses, things weren't so dark. The two catchers' retrenchment path was clearly lit. Moon light splayed from the snow-covered roadway, making everything look surreal. Slowly, with roosters in-hand, never mind the angry flapping wings, they labored. Over the slippery snow, they lugged, load after load of the defiant roosters from house number one to the second house.

When released into house number two, the displaced roosters were peaceful; they quickly assimilated with the flock. No rooster fights broke out, at least until sun up.

The second truck was fully loaded with about twenty eight hundred white rock heavy hens. Puffs of frozen breath billowed from the mouths of the truck workers as they moved about the perimeter of the loaded vehicle, their actions agile and deliberate. As they had with the first truck, they began to secure the chicken coops. Chains were thrown across the stacked coops, chain buckles were set in place, and a tarp was strapped across the front rict. Again, in chorus, the truck workers belted out their loaded truck dialogue. "Head-ache! Chain coming across, boss-man!"

"Let her rip, cowboy!"

But this time a small problem had presented itself. When W.B. Ray, a designated chain buckler, so assigned because of his superior strength, had attempted to cinch one of the chains, the buckle broke. A replacement would be required, because the truck couldn't move until everything was secure. W.B. shuffled off to The Crate. There, he looked under the spare tire, where spare buckles were kept just for such occasions.

When he raised the spare tire and shined the flashlight on the various pieces of hardware, his dark eyes gleamed and a crooked little smile smeared W.B.'s bearded face. He'd discovered something delightful. Amongst the red metal hardware, staring back at him, was an unopened half-pint of Jim Beam. He seated himself, staring at first as though spellbound. Quickly then, he picked up the bottle, broke the seal and took a snort. Twisting his jaw and pursing his lips to one side, W.B. mumbled to himself, "Shreckon Ole Cah'ta boy, won't shrank iss." His words sounded funny, because he was tongue-tied. Drunk or sober, W.B. couldn't talk plainly.

    W.B. took another large swig and swirled the cold liquor from jaw to jaw before swallowing. He cocked his head, then shook it violently. He whistled in cold mountain air and huffed out a warm cloud of liquor-laced breath. Looking about furtively and seeing nothing but his breath, he gulped down another large swallow. Meticulously he capped the bottle and pocketed it inside his green, Army Surplus coat. This time he zipped up the coat, chin-high, something he never did, and turned up his coat collar.

    Then he removed an intact replacement buckle and placed the spare tire back on the floor, exactly as he'd found it. His tracks covered, and fortified by the warming liquor he had filched, W.B. sauntered innocently back to the loaded chicken truck, and finished buckling down the chains. He made very sure he didn't go near anyone or talk to anyone, lest they smell the liquor on his breath.

    Both trucks were now ready to roll, only the roadway was covered in about three inches of snow, and Foreman Frank ordered that snow chains be installed on the truck's traction tires. This was a cold, miserable, solitary task, and W.B. Ray volunteered without hesitation. Frank had already installed chains on The Crate, and W.B. set to work on the loaded truck.

The convoy was finally ready to roll from the North Carolina mountain town. Foreman Frank drove The Crate and led two fully-loaded chicken trucks. The caravan began a slow journey over the snow-covered twisting roads; back to Highway 64; then on to Stiles' Feed Mill in Murphy for weigh out. Meanwhile, the chicken catchers could now take a break and wait for the third truck to arrive. Their biggest problem was how to stay warm, while waiting for that last truck.

W.B. sneaked out of sight, inside the chicken house, ostensibly to get in out of the cold. It was no warmer inside than out, and any perceived warmth was mental rather than physical. Sheets of ice formed in the tops of the chickens' water troughs. With no one in sight, W.B. unzipped his green coat, retrieved his found treasure, and downed a few more snorts. Then he danced around, bouncing from one foot to the other, like a prize fighter, trying to get warm. He finished off the half-pint and flung the bottle to the corner of the chicken house. As he did, the rest of the smoke-blowing crew entered, destroying his privacy.

"Damn man, I'm hungrier 'en a bitch wolf'," moaned Jimmy Wimpey, a spirited older teen. "I could eat a dead horse," came the cry from J.D. Harrison, as he quickly dashed into the house rubbing his hands together.

Enlivened by the booze and now feeling more gregarious, W.B., in tongue-tied words replied, "Hell Shun! Shoin't she bile shum eggs and eats shem? W.B.'s speech impediment caused him to pronounce many words with an "sh" prefix.

"Eggs? You say eggs?"

"Splenty of eggs in shere. Lookies at shem shover in 'shem shest," W.B. countered.

Wimpey walked over to where W.B. had pointed, then called out, "Hell fellers! He's right! Ahe's all kind of eggs in these nests. We could eat em. But we ain't got no way to cook 'em."

W.B. shot back, "shbuilds a shire. Splenty wood out shide."

Pee Wee muttered to another catcher standing beside him, whose teeth were chattering as well, "Fire sounds damn good to me, man! My feet are colder than a well digger's ass. Let's go scrounge up some wood," he proposed. Together the two left, and walked among the silent, snow-coated trees. They gathered up arm loads of wood, breaking and piling it in the road between the two chicken houses.

A fire was lighted from tar paper found inside the chicken house and, within minutes, a roaring orange blaze glowed. Flames crackled and flared, reflecting off the fallen snow. All the chicken catchers encircled the fire. It was a long lost friend, and they held their hands over the flames. Those fortunate enough to have cigarettes or able to bum one, lit them, thanks to a flaming stick lighted by the fire.

A bucket was filled with eggs and ice water, and suspended over the fire by two catchers, who held opposite ends of a slender metal chicken feed trough. The bucket soon boiled. The men occasionally switched tired hands, spilling a little water on the fire each time, alarming the frozen, tired, anxious, definitely hungry catchers.

W.B. watched, but kept silent, with his back turned to the fire. Then he announced to the catchers, "Betcha two dollars shi's eats shmost eggs."

Wimpey countered with, "You're on then. Hell, I'll even go first. I'm starving!"

Side wagers on the chosen winner were made by the other catchers.

The guys who held the boiling bucket of eggs carried it into the snow and set it down. The contents of the bucket were emptied out onto the snow, and steam billowed up, as the eggs sank and the hot water melted the snow. The quickly-cooled feast was gathered and placed in front of Wimpey. Meanwhile, the cooking crew put another pot on to boil. W. B. turned his back to the roaring fire, and kept his silence. Wimpey quickly downed nine eggs, then slowed his eating pace, before finally eating six more eggs. Then he said, "Beat that, Sum Bitch! Fifteen eggs."

W.B. turned around, still saying nothing. He began to peel and eat eggs, throwing the shells to his side and into the fire. An hour later, egg shells encircled him. The shells from thirty-one eggs rested on a bed of snow around him. Only then did he finally break his silence. "How's shminnie shat shmakes shme?"

"Damn, W.B.! You ate thirty-one eggs! And I thought I was hungry," was Wimpey's lament, as he handed W.B. a crisp two dollar bill.

The Crate and the awaited last truck rumbled into sight. The truck was readied for loading; chains were unbuckled, coops were removed and stacked at the back; a make-shift set of steps leading from the ground to the truck's bed level was built with ten coops. Then, in the shivering early dawn hours, the coldest time of day in the North Carolina Mountains, the last of that night's chickens were loaded.

Next, the loose chickens were caught by hand. Surprisingly, they were easy to catch because they didn't try to flee. It was as if they recognized they had nowhere to escape. The snow had incapacitated them.

# SNOWBIRDS

The bad news came just as the new-morning sun first peeped over the rim of the North Carolina mountains. The chicken catchers had scrunched together in the back of the old Dodge panel truck called "The Crate", trying to stay warm. Foreman Frank pushed back his Russian fur hat, exposing a receding hairline that crowned his weary face, with a grimace that clearly screamed, "What now?" He rolled down the driver's side window, ready to receive news he already knew he wasn't going to like. The owner, whose laying hens we'd labored all night to load in the bitter cold, was the messenger. Catchers hushed one another and eavesdropped shamelessly.

"Mr. Crawford called me and told me to tell you to get the crew down to the River Road to a place called Boyd Gap. Said that first truck of chickens ya'll loaded done slid off the road, and tumbled down the mountain side. Said he needed you and the crew to hurry on down there, so you can catch and load those chickens again."

"How's the driver? Is Burton Couch okay?"

"Didn't say. Just said the Sheriff and the Tennessee State Patrol was there. They're trying to figure out how to get that wrecked truck off that mountain side, and how to clean up that mess of chicken coops and scattered chickens Crawford Poultry bought from me. He wants Jack to bring his wrecker. I already told Jack to forget about winching out this last truck. Leave it here for now; can't get down The River Road anyway. Roads are closed between Ducktown and Cleveland."

Frank said nothing. He rolled up the window, re-seated his trademark hat, and The Crate crept away on the snowy road, bound for Murphy. In the back, stiff cold poker cards were dealt and bets were placed. The old truck motored away from Shoal Creek, on to Murphy and to The Miami Café where we'd stop. As we entered this truck stop, famous among truckers for the good eats and friendly waitresses, a red-eyed, but now-sober Bill Carter walked up to greet us. He didn't stop to talk, but continued his trek to The Crate. Bill had been thrown off the crew the previous evening for being drunk and cutting one of the other catchers. He had waited overnight at The Miami, sobering up, and now hoped to hitch a ride home. Frank went to the pay phone to call my brother, Brownie, and get the scoop on the wrecked truck.

When he returned, he told the crew, "All right guys, listen up. I know you're all tired, but I need you all to work some more. You'll be paid double what you made last night, if you work today. We've got to catch and load that first truck of chickens again. This time you'll be loading snowbirds. They're running loose on a mountainside down at Boyd Gap. An empty truck is there now, waiting at the wreck site. Anybody can't work, let me know. I'll have to leave you here at the Miami, and come back and get you home later. Get you something quick to take with you to eat. Don't pay for it. It's on my tab, that is if you're working today."

No one declined the invite to double his money.

"Carter Boy" returned from The Crate with a sour, aggravated look on his face. He joined the crew, then loudly announced, "Which one of you punks took my stash? Now, I had a half pint under that tire in The Crate. Which one of you copped my liquor?"

W.B. Ray was the culprit, but if any of his fellow catchers knew this, they didn't squeal. The crew didn't know about the theft, and thought Carter was making up a dummy claim. Carlie Tankersley, whose boot and forearm had fallen victim to Bill Carter's knife, looked down at his mutilated boot and a cold, wet foot and grinned. His scant hidden smile didn't go unnoticed by ol' Carter Boy, who dashed toward Carlie, but never got there. Foreman Frank grabbed Carter, hauled him up short, and told him, "You start one more thing with my men and I'll call the Law on you! If you want to ride home in The Crate, you best set your ass down! You got me?"

Still staring suspiciously at Carlie, Carter said, "Yeah, I got you, boss man. I ain't gonna start nothing."

Carter sat down at a booth alone. He laid his head on the table until everyone had returned to The Crate. Only then did he follow them. A few minutes later, Foreman Frank stopped at Five Points on Highway 64 where, in cold, no-nonsense words, he issued an order. "This is as far as you're going, Carter. Get out."

Silence set in as The Crate continued on to the wreck site at Boyd Gap.

Beams of red light from atop the Sheriff's cruiser collided with the snowdrifts, causing oddly shaped shadows in the early morning light. Tilted columns of snow rose up from the embankment like angled church steeples. They had been formed by a wrathful, nipping wind passing through the Boyd Gap Mountain pass. Below, straight down the side of the mountain about two hundred feet, lay the wrecked chicken truck.

Chains, red buckles, pieces of wooden chicken coops, and other debris pock-marked the white, slippery slope, tracking the path the tumbling truck had taken. A closer look revealed white chickens dotting the snowy, already cluttered landscape. They appeared stuck, camouflaged, in white quicksand, with only their fluttering wings to give away their positions.

Three men in statuesque poses stood at the top of Boyd Gap overlooking the wreckage. They were the Polk County Sheriff, a Tennessee Highway Patrol officer, and Burton Couch, the driver of the chicken truck. The three surveyed the carnage with disbelief written on their faces. Burton had miraculously managed to jump to safety when the truck started its slide down the mountain.

Burton's face was almost as white as the snow that camouflaged the chickens. He wore no coat; only a shirt and a hunter's cap, and appeared to be in shock. The sun was up, and the frigid wind whistled in the trees. Burton was not aware of the cold.

An empty chicken truck was on the scene. Jack Crawford, my brother, was also there with the wrecker. He stood to the side, studying how to best position the wrecker to winch the tractor and trailer from the bottom of the ravine.

As the catcher crew unloaded, they punched

each other and hurled phony barbs back and forth.

"Hey! W.B.! How Shmany snowbird eggs do you think you could eat?" came Jimmy Wimpey's quip that mocked W.B.'s unique speech.

W.B., true to form, ignored the younger catcher.

Work and chatter came to life. Both weary and cold, the catchers started their work routines, even though few things were routine about catching chickens in the snow. They cursed and belittled each other. Ironically, hidden and certainly never spoken by any chicken catcher, was a true spirit of fellowship. In a strange way, they honored each other's misery. They each ate from the same table of despair. They all worked in the cruel cold to accommodate each other, and get the job done.

The empty truck was readied. Loading snowbirds would be done a little differently. First, coops of chickens that had not been broken in the wreck would be carried up the mountain. With a catcher on either end of the full coop, the men struggled to stand and walk, supporting their shared load. Up the rough and slippery mountain side, together they labored to deliver the chickens to the waiting truck workers. These workers then stacked the cages onto the truck, and this continued, until all the undamaged coops had been removed from the mountainside.

Next, the loose chickens were caught by hand. Surprisingly, they were easy to catch because they didn't try to flee. It was as if they recognized they had nowhere to escape. The snow had incapacitated them. Also, everyone was surprised that so few chickens had been killed outright in the wreck.

Carrying two hands full of snowbirds was not as easy as catching them. The catchers struggled to keep their balance. The mountain was steep. Large, jagged rocks were hidden beneath the snow, causing the catchers to slip and stumble. The frozen snow was cunningly deceptive; at first it seemed it would support a man's weight, but then it would collapse, without warning, causing a catcher with his hands full of chickens to fall. Losing his grip on the chickens, meant the chickens would be loose again. Over and over, until the job was done, the same tired, raw hands would re-catch the same dropped birds, with some being caught three and four times before they were finally captured and cooped.

These chickens had been "banded", meaning a blood test certification band was present on the right leg of each fowl. Though present before, dealing with the bands was now a problem. A raw, wet hand clutching the chicken's snow-coated and banded leg could cause that hand to be sliced open. Catching the left leg was critical for avoiding a razor-sharp cut. Chicken catchers never wore gloves. Doing so could get you labeled as a "girly thang." All of this made gripping the chickens' legs more painful.

We caught and carried chickens up the rough side of Boyd Gap all day, until finally, the truck was loaded. While I looked for any escaped, stray chickens in the silent woods, I happened to look back up the mountain. At the top, I saw Pee Wee in his Sherlock Holmes hat. The sun was sinking behind him. At no one in particular he flashed another of his traditional toothless smiles. He could smile, even though in one bitterly cold night and one dreary day, he had caught the same roosters twice, and many of the same hens several times. He, like the rest of the weather-numbed crew, was beyond being tired, but he was not defeated. We all were proud of the work we had done.

*Times have changed
and people are
so different today.*

GONE

Her life was a sad, tangled mess, much like the hair of the lady in the mirror. She was blind to the new wrinkles on her pale, faded face, however, as she slowly felt of her thin, crimped hair, softly separating the once wanton waves. Picking up her brush, she faintly feigned to recapture what once had been. Her eyes strayed from the mirror, entranced at something only she could see in the distance, and she pondered her situation. Then she flinched and blinked both eyes, winking, if you would, as though the lady in the mirror shared her secret. Puddles of large bags drooped under tired eyes. Baggage so bad, had she been flying today, airport ticketing would have charged her extra to carry them on the plane. Only she wasn't traveling anywhere today; at least nowhere she hadn't been hundreds of times before in her hard luck life. The only flight she would take was confined to the air space of her fanciful confused mind.

"Maybe this is why he left me." This fleeting thought touched down, but then, just as quickly, lifted off and ascended. "His loss!" she quickly assured herself, as she removed a wilted daisy from a nearby vase, and wedged it behind her ear. She recalled her girlhood, remembering fantasies of all the busy bee boys. The ones who saw her as a beautiful flower; the ones whose desires she aroused when she danced with them at the parties she attended as a young girl. Parties were frequent then, and she met her social duty with delight by attending them all. That was then, but this was now. A life of harshness had not, however, given her a hardened attitude. "Times have changed and people are so different today," she muttered as she lay down the worn brush, whose handle flaked its finish coating.

She shuffled over to a tiny closet where she removed an apron, gingerly looping the neck strap over her head, but she didn't tie the side strings. Instead, she held the strings out to either side of her body, stepped lively, and pretended to waltz with a partner, a distinguished gentleman, to be sure. Energized, hand in hand, they glided into the adjoining room, a meagerly furnished living room and kitchenette in a small, upstairs, walk up flat. There she saw her teen son sprawled out on the soiled and faded, lumpy sofa, asleep. Ignoring him totally, she dropped the apron strings and raced to the window, inspired by sounds she'd heard from outside. It was the familiar voice from her past that wafted through the window, that motivated and propelled her. "It's him!" She gushed to herself. "He has no business coming here looking like that," she screeched, clutching her face, but she didn't call his name aloud.

Her outburst awakened the sleeping teen, who raised his head and stared at his mother. He remained silent, however, and watched her ongoing, petulant outburst. Her dark and frantic behavior was familiar, and he knew it all too well. This time it was a bit different; she was more dramatic, more real, he thought. But why? Unbeknownst to him, his mother had fallen to pieces at the sound and then the sight of her ex-husband. The man who had promised her, "Until death do us part." The man with whom she had invested her love and her life for thirty years. Those had been hard, crushing years. Years filled with pain and little joy. There had been more thin times than thick times. Times she had never been accustomed to as a young woman of affluence. He was just a regular guy from a family of modest means, but he had exceptionally good looks. His charm and gift of persuasion had made her an easy prey. Financial success had somehow eluded their married life, maybe because they both had wanted something more than just wealth. Raising a large family together had made their chosen "road less traveled;" a hardscrabbled road of want and comfort denied.

"I'll show him I've moved on with my life!" she mumbled angrily. She raced back to her bedroom, where she grabbed her newest dress-- new to her, but long out of style and in dire need of pressing. She returned to the mirror and again faced the lady with whom she shared her secret. Frizzing, teasing and applying make-up and burgundy lipstick, she emerged as a new person. "I wonder if he'd know me now?" she asked herself, then raced to peek again from the window. "Where is he?" she demanded. Her young teen son sat up now, scrutinized his mom's new appearance, and wondered at her energized demeanor. Her flurry of ecstatic activity puzzled him. What could she possibly have to be happy about? He reflected over what was happening, but remained silent.

She thought to herself, "This can't be a coincidence. He knows we live here. Maybe he just took a wrong turn or he got the wrong house number. I'll give him a clue; I'll play our favorite dance music, the songs we sometimes danced to at home, alone, when the children were sleeping.

Dashing across the room, she uncased a vintage 33-1/3 vinyl record. The artists, "The Platters" were featured on the front of the dusty, old, dog-eared cover. "Music civilized people can move to and express themselves with," she told herself. She snapped her fingers and began moving her hips and feet in the art of the dance, but her jerky motions belied the feel of the slow, mellow music blaring from the antique turntable.

The son, still a bit bewildered, studied the side show his mother was acting out. He recalled having once seen her dancing with his dad. Both had frolicked gracefully together. It was a cherished memory, and was the only time he'd ever seen any love or levity between his parents. Serious concerns now displaced his fond memory. Why was she solo cloud jumping, obviously delusional with happiness?' He rubbed his face, arose, and walked to the window. Looking out he saw a blue sky autumn day. He also saw his dad's car, the car his dad had let him steer when he was a child, while seated on his father's lap. This was the same car in which he'd passed his driver's test not so very long ago. The light bulb started to glow.

He left the window. Her actions now started to make sense, but the flurry of feelings he felt left him suddenly angry. He knew fully well what was going on, as she pretended to dance to the outdated old folks music. "Stop it, Mom! Just stop it! I know what you think you're doing. It's not going to work. He's GONE and he's never coming back!"

"What are you talking about, son," she replied, her face a picture of confusion. In her ear, she could hear and feel the guilt that laced her voice. Her blissful face didn't jibe with the truth her voice betrayed. "Who's not coming back?

"Dad's not coming back. He hates us, but he hates you more. Why did you make him leave us?" her son demanded, anger prominent in his voice and body language.

"Son, you don't know what you're talking about. I didn't divorce your dad. He divorced me. Then he left town with that bony blonde bitch. I didn't divorce him, and I don't know why he chose to come here today."

"No, Mom, you may not have run him off, but you made it impossible for him to live with us. You were always getting mad and leaving us at home all alone. Why did you do that? Why did you leave us like that, Mom?"

"He was mean to me!" she snarled. "Your daddy was mean to me. He said awful things and h-h-he... he never once brought me flowers," she cried triumphantly. A man shouldn't treat a lady the way your dad treated me. And--and-- he hit me once when I refused to stop talking. He hit me! That's why I left you all. He--h--he was mean to me." Then she broke into uncontrollable tears and raced to her bedroom, slamming the door closed behind her. Her shrill cries of anguish muffled and muted the soft melodies emerging from the old spinning piece of black vinyl.

The boy walked over to the window and looked down at the street again. This time he saw his dad, a gray, slim built, distinguished looking man, standing by the family car. He signaled with a wave of his hand that he would be right down. A nod of his Dad's head acknowledged the silent message. Then the boy turned from the window, walked to his mom's room, and knocked on her door.

He entered the room, but she chose to ignore him. Still, he wouldn't be deterred, as he announced, "Mom, here's your pill. Please take your medicine before I go. You need this to stay balanced. I'll be back tomorrow. I'm taking Dad for his first chemo treatment today, but I'll come back on my lunch break tomorrow, to check in on you." He leaned over her bed, planted a kiss on her tear-traced, powdered cheek, then turned and walked away. She continued sobbing, still ignoring his presence.

As he descended the stairs to street level, the old spinning black vinyl record began the closing song by the Platters...

"They said someday you'll find
All who love are blind
Oh, when your heart's on fire
You must realize
Smoke Gets In Your Eyes."

"Now laughing friends deride
Tears I cannot hide
So I smile and say
When a lovely flame dies
Smoke gets in your eyes."

Now with a house payment,
a station wagon payment,
and several other 'necessary
things for the girls',
the years flew by.
The couple lived
the American dream.

 # BOUNDEN

Life ends for all, and relationships fall apart and go in different directions, but love and the memories of that love are eternal. Can I define Love? No. Like Forrest Gump, I'm not a smart man, but I do know what love is when I see it. Sometimes silent, sometimes invisible, and often obscure, it does exist and will always prevail.

"I once witnessed love lived out loud. When compared to eternity, the couple were together for only a sliver of time. Their love began and thrived in hard times in an unlikely place, a small remote copper mining community, known as the twin cities of McCaysville, Georgia and Copperhill, Tennessee."

In their youth, World War II changed everything for them. America "had God on its side," but fear and uncertainty persisted. A Government Observatory Corp Post in the Copper Basin made all who lived there very mindful of the precarious times. The war threatened and influenced every life. Like an earthquake, it first destroyed, but then redirected their young hopes and dreams. The war caused this couple's first years together to be far from typical. War and love are alike in that one respect: nothing is ever typical in war or love.

She had it all. Smart. Athletic. With Rita Hayworth good looks to boot. Salutatorian of her graduating high school class and captain of the basketball team, her senior year grade average was 90.1. Maybe that's not all that amazing until one considers that she took both the Junior AND Senior year classes at the same time. War gave a sense of urgency to everything and everyone. She was driven to succeed, and would have been accepted without difficulty in any school of nursing or teaching. These were the two acceptable professions for women of the 1940's. She chose neither.

He was the oldest of three sons. Reserved and handsome, sporting springtime sky blue eyes, dark skin, and black wavy hair. His parents, like hers, were longtime residents of the twin cities area. His dad worked as a miner in the Copper Mines of Copperhill, Tennessee. After being diagnosed with Silicosis, his dad left the mines and opened a grocery store in McCaysville, Georgia. All of the brothers were good students, participated in sports, and were no strangers to daily chores. Like most young men of the area, they were patriotic and ready to join their buddies when the call to war came.

He and his younger brother served during World War II. The youngest brother later served in the Korean Conflict. Their mom prayed daily for her sons' safe return from the battlefield. Unlike most War Mothers during WW II, she didn't place her Blue Star Flag in her window. She needed no symbol to remind her of the sacrifices a war demanded. Instead, she cherished and preserved the flag, putting it away for safe keeping. Today, the faded seventy year old red flag with two blue stars screams the message to those who would hear: Love prevailed.

They married just before he joined the Army, and for thirty months, they were separated by the war. She waited, worried, and longed for his return. Letters were exchanged, but were often long-delayed in delivery. He did his basic training at Camp Robinson in Little Rock, Arkansas, and was stationed in Tulla Homa, Tennessee, before being sent to Germany, where he served as a Medic. Because of a physical ailment, he had been assigned to a non-combat role with the battlefield sawbones. He had unstable blood pressure; the insidious ailment had surfaced during basic training. Since every able-bodied man was needed, he was placed in the company of medical professionals, near the front lines of fighting.

Though he saw no combat, he helped treat many soldiers who were injured in battle and afterward, he was always reluctant to share those things he'd seen. When asked about his time in the military, he often ignored the question. Sometimes, tongue in cheek, he'd emphatically reply, "I wouldn't take a million dollars for the time I spent in the Army." Then, almost too quickly, he'd glibly add, "And I wouldn't give one red cent for another day of it." Once, when Vietnam War protests were prevalent, he told me about something he saw while stationed at Tulla Homa. Even thirty years later, the words he'd read on a sign at the entrance to a restaurant still disturbed him. Troubled, angry eyes became misty as he rubbed a rough hand through his receding white hair. Quietly he said, "That sign read, 'Soldiers and dogs not welcome inside.'" Love prevailed.

Like so many other young couples after the war ended, they wanted a house and a family. He was employed by the Tennessee Copper Company, where he first worked as a day laborer. Later, he served a carpenter's apprenticeship. After work each day, working together, timber by timber, side by side, the couple labored to build their home; a home they lived in for life. The land for the house was a small lot, a gift from her daddy. Many exhausting evenings and plenty of sweat was invested in their dream home.

After they moved into the house they'd built, she became pregnant, but didn't carry the baby to term. She was devastated by the miscarriage, and the loss it represented, and by feelings of utter failure as a woman, a wife, and mother. Together, with kindness from caring friends and family, they got through the loss. Love prevailed.

Two years later, on an unusually cold May morning, they were blessed with a child. The baby was delivered in their home by Dr. Thomas Jugarthy Hicks, thought by some in the Copper Basin to be the devil incarnate, because he sold the babies of unwed mothers. Others considered him to be a candidate for sainthood, because he strived to help all, regardless of their ability to pay. But at the conclusion of his house call, a healthy baby, a beautiful little blond-headed girl, was the reward. Two years later, her little sister entered the world kicking and screaming at Cook's Hospital.

Now with a house payment, a station wagon payment, and several other 'necessary things for the girls', the years flew by. The couple lived the American dream. She was a stay-at-home mom. She taught Sunday-School, Girl's Auxiliary, and was active in the PTA and other local functions. Always the athlete, she played in the women's softball league in the summer, and bowled in the winter. By hand, she made most all of the clothes worn by their daughters.

He was the breadwinner. Full of faith and dreams, he was determined to provide well for his family, so he worked two jobs. He was also active in his church, served as a deacon, and was constantly doing volunteer carpentry projects. She once became tired of his constant absence from home, and resented all the time he donated to the church. "Wait a minute," she once demanded of him as he was leaving home for the church to work. She then retreived a sleeping cot from the closest, handed it to him and said, "Take this with you to the church to sleep on. It'll save you travel time. You stay there more than here at home."

One thing each family member wanted was a boat. He indulged that desire. She and the daughters spent time together with friends on Blue Ridge Lake. These were the happiest days of the family's life. In the summer, the family pitched a tent and lived on the lake. They came home only to attend church on Sundays and Wednesday nights.

Fishing and bird hunting were his and her "away together time." This shared time was therapeutic. She was an aficionado of these two hobbies, once thought to be for men only. Together, they drowned worms, trolled lake shores, and fished out solutions. Life's problems fluttered away like stalked quail when King, their working bird dog, held point. Skies were made blue again.

Their family pet dog, named Duchess, loved two things: the two little girls and the popcorn each would feed her. Duchess was a pious pup and very religious.

She was also serious about church attendance, and always ran to nearby Kingtown Baptist Church, where the family attended. She would wait patiently for them in the parking lot. On one occasion, however, Duchess sneaked inside the church, walked to the altar, lay down in front of the pulpit, and listened attentively as he gave the church's financial report. Giggles and sniggers erupted when she became bored, gave a large yawn and a yap. He flawlessly finished his report, totally ignoring his devout detractor.

Time marched toward destiny and the parents of both passed away. Her mother's sickness and death was a lingering, protracted ordeal. She had Arterial Sclerosis and symptoms of Alzheimer's. For seven years she was her mama's caretaker. For most of those years, her mother didn't know her or recognize anyone else. To test her memory, I was once introduced to her mama as being the Fuller Brush Man. At this stage of the disease, the older woman didn't know me either.

Her mother's many years of sickness took an emotional and psychological toll on her, and the fear of being like her mama in her own later years haunted her. She soldiered on. Love prevailed.

He was a dedicated employee of the Tennessee Copper Company. In his mind, missing a day's work was just plain wrong. After twenty years he received a wristwatch with an inscription on the back that read:

> PRESENTED BY
> TENNESSEE COPPER COMPANY
> IN APPRECIATION OF
> LOYAL SERVICE
> 1946 - 1966

Forty-seven years later, his daughter, an Elementary School Principal, proudly wears her dad's watch. She too, never misses a day at work.

After an international corporation acquired the Copper Company, he continued to receive recognition awards for his faithful service. When he was fifty-six he had worked in the same place for over thirty-five years, only now he was a foreman. Times, they changed.

The following year, the corporation terminated him. Swept him into the wind like an old, has-been brown leaf. The new corporation had a "bottom-line first" management philosophy. Corporate stockholders came first. Stakeholders were now less important. At age fifty-six, he was too old to do physically demanding construction work. Yet he was too young to retire. He had to have a job. The real problem was that no other employers existed in this "one-company town." Love prevailed.

He took his circumstances as a challenge and

promptly adjusted. He and a work buddy formed a partnership. Together they remodeled houses. Work that was hard and painful in his autumn years. Having high blood pressure was also risky for the type work he did, but he was no quitter. He never complained. Only once did I ever hear him hint at a complaint, when he lamented, "Seven of the last ten remodeling jobs I've done have been bathroom remodeling jobs. I hate bathroom jobs." He shook his head, but said nothing more.

He soldiered on and made it to early retirement age. Now, with a fixed income, he could do more of what they both enjoyed, watching the Atlanta Falcons and the Atlanta Braves on TV. He could also spend more time with his grandkids. One treat he and the grandsons enjoyed weekly was hauling off the trash to the landfill. There, on the back roads, he allowed them to drive his old pickup truck. Sometimes, with a twenty-two rifle or a Bee-Bee gun, they would "thin out" the rat population.

He was a peculiar man in many ways. She would be the first to tell you, "He's stubborn as a mule and sometimes he makes me so mad, I can't see straight." I once asked her, "Did you ever think of divorcing him?" She looked at me like I'd just gotten off a spacecraft from Mars, but then smiled and said, "No, but I've thought about shooting him once or twice."

He projected a gruff persona. His hands were always rough, but his heart was tender. In the war he'd seen death and was especially sensitive to people going through a death in their family. Sometimes he'd fake some gallows humor about his deacon duty of attending funeral wakes. He'd say, "Well, I got to go out to the funeral home. They got old so and so covered up with flowers, and he's 'On Display' out there."

He was also skeptical of doctors and would not seek medical attention whenever he was sick. He self-diagnosed and self-treated most of his ailments. Aspirin and Four-Way-Cold medicine were the only drugs he took. Once I encouraged him to go see a doctor. He stormed back at me, "Doctors take your money; they tell you they don't know, or tell you something you already know. So, why go?"

He was visiting us when I first sensed that he was sicker than he pretended not to be. He'd stopped to rest while walking from the car to the front door, a distance of less than one hundred feet. I asked, "Are you all right?" He responded, "I'm okay. I'll be on in the house in a few minutes." Two days later, he was dead. That hideous high blood pressure had caught up with him. Like a light bulb, he had gone out, leaving the physical world behind. A massive heart attack; the doctor he had avoided would have told us.

Today, a family life center stands beside the

church, near the cemetery where he's buried, and where he had donated so many hours. A memorial plaque was hung in the center to honor his devotion and service to his church.

When he died, life got colder for her. She no longer was "a hot head" as he'd sometimes called her. Mortality was made more clear, and she wondered how long before she'd join him. Until then, she would live in a brave new world. In their marriage, he had done it all. Handled the finances, home repairs, and dealt with all the little emergencies. She never even balanced a checkbook before his death. Learning and adapting at age sixty-four was tough, but she had always been a quick study. Love prevailed.

Today, she lives alone in the home that they built together, timber by timber; the home where they raised their family; the home in which many of her memories were made. Her five brothers and one sister have all passed on. Her circle of friends at church gets smaller with each passing year. She still enjoys an intellectual challenge. She works puzzles, reads books, and edits some of my writings. At eighty-seven, she's forgotten more English than most college graduates know. Mostly, she reads the Holy Bible, but will always take a break to watch a sports event on TV.

Her love affair with sports has never faded. Not so long ago, she called me to ask what time she should set her alarm clock. She wanted to be up in time to watch the Wimbledon Tennis Championship game, a game being televised from England at ten a.m.

Today, she has Arnold Chiari Syndrome, a disease that robs her memory. She gets angry with herself because she's not as articulate as she once was. She also has pain when walking, caused by a once broken foot. She begrudgingly walks with a cane; she sees it as a token of old age and doesn't like it even a little bit. In one leg she has arthritis. That's the leg she broke playing in a pick up football game with teenage boys. Even though she was forty-eight years old at the time, the boys all agreed she was a true gamer and showed potential for becoming a great run-and-gun quarterback.

Every week she phones to check on how her great-grand kids are doing; wants to know their progress in school and sports. She gives a report on the latest "goings on" in her world that is the twin cities of McCaysville, Georgia, and Copperhill, Tennessee.

The treasures from the copper mines have long been mined out. Both towns are now retirement communities and a popular stop for a tourist train. For her, both towns are unchanged and love abides there. She's duty bounden and determined to see that the memories stay.

Love prevails.

About the Author

Joe Cobb Crawford, PE, is a native on the tri-state area of Georgia, Tennessee, and North Carolina, the setting and material source for his third book. A hampered student who quit school three times, he married at age seventeen, but became a scholar and graduated with honors from Southern Technical Institute in Marietta, Georgia, and holds a MS degree in engineering from the University of Tennessee in Knoxville. Joe is a licensed professional engineer in numerous southeastern states.

Today he trains people in electrical engineering, safety, and energy conservation initiatives. He is a Senior Member of the Institute of Electrical and Electronics Engineers, and he works with the IEEE to develop electrical safety design standards.

He resides on Lake Hartwell near Toccoa, Georgia, with his wife of forty-five years, Susan, an elementary school principal. Joe credits faith, family and those early lessons he learned from the most unlikely souls of God's humanity, his fellow "Chicken Catchers," as the inspiration for his life's accomplishments and the wellhead from which his stories are drawn.

See what Joe's readers are saying. Add your comments to The Poetry Company Readers page on Facebook, or visit the website below.

http://www.crawfordpoetrycompany.com

About the Artist

Ken Woodall is a folk artist with a rare talent – he remembers clearly things from long ago. He masterfully captures images of southern culture that evoke memories of yesteryear. His vibrant one-of-a-kind paintings transport viewers back in time and remind them of their departed heritage.

In Northeast Georgia near the Chattahoochee in Habersham County, Ken collected his first rural memories of the South. College, work, and raising a family postponed his life's dream to become an artist, but he continued to collect memories. Years later after traveling throughout the Southeast on business, Ken pursued his dream of being an artist. His collected memories spanned half a century and he now has a vast array of southern memories to recall. He paints cultural events and the changes witnessed over the middle part of the twentieth century. A southern style Americana of that era is expressed with unforgettable features in his paintings.

Proof of Ken's unique style and content can be seen throughout the Southeast. Galleries in Highlands, N.C., Augusta, Georgia, and Atlanta, Georgia collect Ken's art. His paintings hang on the walls of Georgia's Capital Building and Emory Hospital. Other notable Georgia collectors of Ken's work are former governor of Georgia, Carl Sanders, Anne Cox Chambers, and Cabbage Patch Kid creator, Xavier Roberts. New York City residents also treasure Ken's work. Each Memorial Day, Ken and his wife Corinne travel to Greenwich Village to display his latest paintings in the Washington Square Art Exhibit.

View a sample of Ken's paintings
by visiting the website below:

http://www.mountainfolkartist.com/about.html

If you enjoyed

Mountain Shadow Memories

Be sure to read Joe's other two books:

When The Chickens Come Home To Roost

and

**The Poetry Company:
Memoirs of a Chicken Catcher**

Available where fine southern books are sold

www.crawfordpoetrycompany.com